SURVIVING THE TRUTH

—

TYLER ANNE SNELL

D0980822

⟨H⟩HARLEQUIN
INTRIGUE

This book is for Hannah, Ace, Madi and Kelvin. Writing this
book came at a very stressful time for the Tyler household, and
you all were nothing but kind to us. Roll Tide (sorry, Madi)!

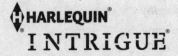

HARLEQUIN®
INTRIGUE®

Recycling programs
for this product may
not exist in your area.

ISBN-13: 978-1-335-48908-1

Surviving the Truth

Copyright © 2021 by Tyler Anne Snell

This edition published by arrangement with Harlequin Books S.A.

For questions and comments about the quality of this book,
please contact us at CustomerService@Harlequin.com.

Harlequin Enterprises ULC
22 Adelaide St. West, 40th Floor
Toronto, Ontario M5H 4E3, Canada
www.Harlequin.com

Printed in U.S.A.

Tyler Anne Snell genuinely loves all genres of the written word. However, she's realized that she loves books filled with sexual tension and mysteries a little more than the rest. Her stories have a good dose of both. Tyler lives in Alabama with her same-named husband and their mini "lions." When she isn't reading or writing, she's playing video games and working on her blog, *Almost There*. To follow her shenanigans, visit tylerannesnell.com.

Books by Tyler Anne Snell

Harlequin Intrigue

The Saving Kelby Creek Series

Uncovering Small Town Secrets
Searching for Evidence
Surviving the Truth

Winding Road Redemption

Reining in Trouble
Credible Alibi
Identical Threat
Last Stand Sheriff

The Protectors of Riker County

Small-Town Face-Off
The Deputy's Witness
Forgotten Pieces
Loving Baby
The Deputy's Baby
The Negotiation

Manhunt
Toxin Alert

Visit the Author Profile page at Harlequin.com.

CAST OF CHARACTERS

Kenneth Gray—This widower comes back to the Dawn County Sheriff's Department as the lead of a new cold-case unit. He's ready to give justice to those who deserve it after the corruption that tore through the town leaves more questions than answers. But when an intriguing woman pleads with him to help her solve a decades-old cold case, his main priority becomes keeping her safe.

Willa Tate—After finding a box buried at one of her work sites, this amateur sleuth uncovers what she believes to be an unsolved murder over thirty years old. Unable to close the case on her own, she enlists the help of a detective who refuses to bend to threats and swears that she'll be safe as long as they're together.

Ally Gray—Kenneth's deceased wife, who has also become one of the unit's cold cases, may be more connected to the danger than anyone realizes.

Martha Tate-Smith—Willa's little sister and her husband, Kimball, do whatever they can to help out when the situation gets dangerous.

Josiah Linderman—A man who Willa believes was murdered thirty-five years ago when he disappeared without a trace.

Prologue

"The conclusion I've come to is an easy one, even if it is a frustrating one." Detective Lovett dropped the box on the sheriff's desk. It landed with a notable thud. "We need help—and I'm talking specific help, not just me and an unlimited supply of coffee."

Sheriff Chamblin let out a breath that sank his shoulders and protruded his belly. He was at his desk but wasn't happy about it. He was a man who liked to pound the pavement, not pour over paperwork. Plus, with the way things had ebbed and flowed from quiet to downright loud in Kelby Creek throughout the last year or so, it was hard to feel at ease anywhere, most notably behind a desk.

So Chamblin hadn't been in the best of moods before the detective had come in and now, with Lovett's conclusion, he feared it wasn't going to get any better.

Chamblin spelled out the obvious. "You want the task force."

Lovett nodded. "Normally a place so small wouldn't need one, but given Kelby Creek's history, there're a lot more cold cases that we need to look into. Ones that we thought were resolved but weren't. Ones that we thought we had the right person for but—"

"But we don't," Chamblin finished. He sighed again and motioned to the box. "We have enough of these cases for an actual task force? What does that even entail? Two people? Four? How would you have handled this in Seattle?"

The detective thumbed at his wedding band and shrugged.

"In Seattle we would have had more than enough people to switch their gears, but here?" He thought a moment. "I'm going to suggest that eventually we have two people but, considering we don't have people lining up to fill the department at the moment, I'd say try for one first. See how that goes. Worst case, it's a glorified trial period. Best case, it does what the rest of us are trying to do."

Chamblin snorted. "And what's that exactly?"

Detective Lovett smiled but didn't return the sarcasm.

"Make the town trust this department again, one good deed at a time." He tapped the box, his expression turning serious. "They're not the only ones who deserve justice."

The sheriff couldn't disagree.

"Whoever we hire, they'll need to be above reproach," he said. "Because if they're anything but trustworthy and straightforward, this town will eat them alive. It's one thing to do right by Kelby Creek when things pop up. It's another to dive into the past and muck around. Whoever does that is going to have their work more than cut out for them."

Lovett nodded. Then he pulled out a piece of paper with a name and number written on it. He passed it over to the sheriff. "That is why I think we should reach out to him."

Chamblin had to read the name twice. Just so he knew he wasn't mistaken. "You've gotta be kidding me."

Detective Lovett shrugged. "Find me a more motivated individual and I'll recommend them instead."

After a moment, Chamblin admitted defeat.

"It'll take some talking to get him back into law enforcement after what happened. And I'm not sure talking will even do anything. We talk about righting the wrongs of this department's past, but there's not a thing we can do to right the wrong of what happened to him."

Lovett's expression softened.

"He's good people and, no matter how life beats good people down, they always find a time to stand right back up." He thumped the piece of paper on the desk twice. "He'll take the job. I bet my badge on it."

There was only one way to find out.

The sheriff picked up the phone and dialed the number. It rang as he traced the name on the paper for the third time.

Kenneth Gray was either about to be intrigued or really, really angry.

Chapter One

Willa Tate wouldn't have found the box at all had she not been trying to be polite.

See, it was a curse—being polite—one she'd been saddled with from a young girl and was still burdened with at the age of thirty-one. Like a bad perm or a wine stain sitting on a white blouse for too long, being polite wasn't just something she decided to do on a daily basis. It was something she *had* to do.

It was in her DNA.

So when Missy Frye called the office in a fuss, worried over her husband and why he wasn't yet home, Willa glanced around the empty space and nodded to no one but herself.

"I can run out to the site to see if he's already gone for the day," she offered, looking for her purse.

Normally it hung on a hook next to her office door, but today she'd gone for fun lunch and, after fun lunch, her purse had a way of landing anywhere but where it was supposed to. Thanks in no small part to her friend and coworker Ebony Keller.

Fun lunch often included a good deal of gossip,

even if no one had asked for it originally. And gossip in small-town Kelby Creek? Well, that wasn't something you just left at the lunch table.

Ebony had hustled into the office, pulling on Willa's side as she'd hurriedly whispered about the newest piece of juice in town. That meant her purse had probably landed near where Ebony had dropped her two cents on what was happening over at the Dawn County Sheriff's Department.

"Oh, Willa, that would be *amazing* of you," Missy nearly yelled back, her accent a brand of Scarlet O'Hara's in *Gone With the Wind*.

Willa's ran a bit deeper and with a lot more syrup. Her family had been in the Deep South town of Kelby Creek for four generations. It was a running joke that by the time Willa had a kid and then that kid had their own, the poor soul would have an accent so thick that no one would be able to understand a word.

"I normally wouldn't even call up there," Missy added, "but Dave usually answers his phone and now it's going straight to voice mail."

"I bet he's just lost track of time is all." Willa tried to assure her. "Give me five minutes and I'll have him calling with an apology on the tip of his tongue."

Missy showered Willa with a few more thank-yous, and even threw in a "Tell your sister I said hi," then the phone was in the cradle and Willa was shaking her head.

She dug into her purse, which had wound up halfway beneath the worn love seat that had catered to many a tired worker, and pulled her personal cell phone out to make sure no one was missing her.

They weren't.

Willa sighed at the lack of notifications and locked up the office with a grumble. Up until a few months ago, she would have had one to ten messages from Landon. But, she supposed, it made sense that they would stop on account of his new—and quick-as-a-flare-up-in-an-unattended-grease-pan—engagement.

Not that Willa was holding that against him.

She *had* been the one to call it quits after all.

You also would have married him had he asked, she pointed out to herself.

Willa shook her head. "No time for feeling any type of way on that," she said aloud. "Now's the time for finding Dave."

Kelby Creek, Alabama, was caught in an awkward way lately. Mostly it had to do with the weather. There was enough humidity to keep Willa's blond hair big and unruly but enough chill to make her wish she'd worn something other than a short-sleeved blouse. Or at least had brought a rain jacket with her. She could smell the rain in the air even if the darkening sky was free of clouds. Late October in south Alabama was a mixed bag when it came to knowing what to be grumpy about when you stepped outside. Today was no exception.

The second way Kelby Creek felt a bit strange was a lot more subtle and, if you weren't a local, harder to pin down. Willa had come to town when she was a teen and had, somehow, managed to not leave it since. She had some feelings on that front but her time in the out-of-pocket place had given her a sensitivity to it. Like most locals, she'd been upset at what had happened two years ago. Hurt. Scared.

Angry.

But now? Now, there was something in the air. Change.

Was it good? Or was it more of the same?

She couldn't tell and most locals couldn't decide, either.

They felt the wind blowing, in a manner of speaking, and no matter which way it would eventually go, it was there all the same.

But, for Willa, she didn't think she would have to ponder on any of that anytime soon. In the grand scheme of town, she wasn't exactly top-tier important. She worked as an office manager for a construction company that catered to all of Dawn County, lived in the garage apartment of her younger sister and husband's house, and had a five-year plan that she'd already extended twice. Willa wasn't the kind of woman to be a part of the important things—the things that made ripples and waves. She was more of the person who watched the troublemakers throw the rocks into the water in the first place.

It was her lot in life and she'd accepted it. Accepted it all the way to the north side of town and right onto a makeshift lot where their workers had been parking to walk to the land they were prepping. Eventually, the lot would be bulldozed, flattened and smoothed. Then it would be turned into a small set of town houses. Right now, there were still a few trees, weeds and dirt mounds interspersed with the construction equipment.

Willa got out of her car and took in most of the area without having to do much. Dave's truck wasn't around and neither was he. Still, Willa had known the man for years and the possibility of him leaving his phone behind at a site was up there with a pretty dang good chance. So she decided to stay polite and do a quick pass over the lot, all while switching her heels for her rain boots and bringing out the light of her phone.

Dave was probably on his way home now after chatting too long with Marvin after work. He'd get an earful from Missy for sure, but maybe Willa could soften the blow by dropping off his misplaced phone.

The first half of the lot still had a few patches of mud from last night's rain. It squished against her boots and made her hurry so she could minimize how much gunk she'd have to wash off when she got home.

Her trek brought her to the back end of the lot, which still had some trees not yet bulldozed, with half attention. When the light of her phone split between a tree, an old stump, and a half-buried rectangle, Willa moved over a few steps, passing it off as a wayward toolbox.

But then, why was it partially buried? Even with a heavy rain, it wouldn't sink underground.

So Willa went back, out of curiosity, already assuming it was some other construction-related thing.

However, it wasn't.

Willa knelt next to the wooden box. Her light showed it was worn, with cracks and matted dirt and mud. Some of the box looked a bit crushed and the metal clasp on the front was off the hinges. She propped her phone up against the tree stump and used both hands to free the box from the dirt. Not heavy enough that she couldn't move it, it definitely required two hands.

"You better not be some kind of *Jumanji* game where I get cursed by opening you," Willa muttered to the box.

It had been a joke.

A silly little thing to say in the dark to herself.

Yet, once she lifted the top, Willa's veins filled with ice.

"Oh my God!"

NOVEMBER BROUGHT IN late tropical storms to Southern Alabama and, with the second, an almost oppressive humidity followed directly by a blanket cold. That was why Kenneth Gray came into the Dawn County Sheriff's Department with his own haul in tow. It was less "make you sweat, cuss, and wish you lived someplace where the seasons stayed in their respective lanes" and more of his only chance of surviving the day.

It was Monday morning and Kenneth entered through the back of the building after swiping his card. He dropped his coffee cup on his desk and the pack of sinus meds next to it. He'd also brought something else that had nothing to do with the headache brewing in the back of his head. That was also why he'd hustled behind closed doors to his desk and not taken any time to talk about the weekend.

That "something else" knew the drill and whipped under the desk to the bed he'd already taken the time to set up his first week on the job. If he had been working anywhere else, he was sure it would be grounds for a firing.

Yet Kelby Creek had been forced to become forgiving. Along with the interim sheriff and the department that served it.

Plus, it wasn't like he brought his dog to work every day.

"Good girl, Delilah," Kenneth said to the three-year-old golden retriever. He pulled a chew toy from his bag and tossed it next to her as she settled.

In Kenneth's opinion, she was the only thing that fit nicely in the room. Everything else around them was mild chaos. The desk that butted his didn't have a chair behind it, but its top was covered in paperwork that had been shifted over from his side. There were boxes and filing cabinets in the room crowding both, and the smallest of placards on the door that still read Storage.

It wasn't supposed to be an office but it had become his.

Just as the cases stacked around him had.

A knock on the door had Delilah sit at attention though Kenneth knew she wouldn't move unless he said so. Still, he tried to block her from view of a man with red hair and crinkles at the edges of his eyes. He had a badge on his uniform and a scowl on his face.

Deputy Carlos Park shook his head in greeting.

"Smart to use the back door. Did you see the line that's out there in the lobby?"

Kenneth shook his head but hadn't missed the more than usual number of cars in the parking lot.

"Is it the same as last week?"

Park nodded. "Ever since the press conference, you, my dude, have stirred up a lot of chatter in town." He pointed at the wall, in the direction of the department's lobby. "Now that chatter has turned into a roomful of people sure as spit simmering on a sidewalk in summer they have information that can solve one of these cold cases."

Kenneth sighed. "If only it was that easy, I wouldn't have this job in the first place."

They each took a moment to glance around the room. Kenneth had known Carlos for years, but just as a passing hello, a quick conversation in the bank line or a how's-it-going while closing out tabs at the bar. But Kenneth had heard of Carlos's feats of excitement over the last two to three years and how the guy had gone from a sour-faced, angry man to a more calm and caring one. As the deputy's gaze swept over the papers and boxes, he wondered if that new side of compassion helped him see what Kenneth saw instead when he looked around.

People.

A void that couldn't be filled but could be stitched closed to make a scar instead of a wound.

However, that was a deeper conversation for another day. No sooner had Carlos's gaze moved across the space did it travel to Kenneth's desk. Or, really, the bright-eyed pup beneath it.

He cracked a grin. "I know you're having some work done on your house but I still think the sheriff will lose it if he sees Delilah here."

Kenneth wasn't that worried.

"That press conference didn't just put me in the public eye, it pushed him out there, too," he reminded the deputy. "I haven't seen the sheriff for more than a few minutes here and there, and that's usually in the break room." He paused and looked at the dog in question. Delilah must have sensed the new thoughtful attention. Her tail started to wag. "That said, give me a heads-up if you see him around."

Carlos laughed and agreed. Then he was back to annoyed. "You going to the conference room for another round of conspiracy theories?"

"I am."

Kenneth sighed, took some of his sinus meds, gave Delilah a pat, and followed the deputy out and to the room next door. Carlos didn't enter, but there was sympathy now written across his face. Someone was already seated at the end of the conference table. Carlos lowered his voice so only Kenneth could hear him. "Good luck, Detective."

Kenneth didn't say so but he didn't believe in luck when it came to Kelby Creek.

Not after what had happened.

Not after Ally had died.

Murdered, not died.

Carlos didn't seem to note the anger and resentment that had burned through Kenneth at the thought. Instead he went off down the hall, unaware the rising frustration that went along with the familiar emotions was only about to be stoked by Kelby Creek residents who liked drama a little too much.

He took a small beat, pulled on a polite smile, and

settled in the chair opposite his first of, he assumed, many locals who wanted a piece of the new cold case task force and the only man heading it.

That polite smile nearly slipped off altogether as Kenneth met the gaze of a woman who was not at all what he'd expected would make his life a little more difficult that Monday morning.

Sunshine.

It was the first descriptor that came to his mind as he quickly took her in.

Shoulder-length, big blond hair, freckles across her face, dark lipstick along her polite expression, and bright green eyes that seemed to be smiling, too. She was petite yet there was no doubt by her curves and demeanor that she was late twenties to early thirties. Her outfit helped drive that conclusion home. A dark red blazer with a blouse tucked in. A gold locket around her neck. Her nails were also immaculately kept. She didn't just care about her appearance, it was most likely a requirement for a job or career.

There was also the other thing that made Kenneth place the woman older than what he might have had they met under different circumstances.

Something was weighing on her.

Something, he guessed, having to do with the wooden box placed on the table between them.

"Good morning," he greeted, keeping his gaze locked on the almost-lime green of her stare until he knew more about why she was there. "I'm Detective Gray. How can I help you?"

The woman's smile went megawatt. She extended her hand so fast he almost flinched.

"Nice to meet you!" Her voice was surprisingly chipper for someone who seemed troubled. Then again, this was the South, and Southern women had a sneaky way about them. They only let you see what they wanted you to see and, right now, the woman wanted to act like she wasn't in a sheriff's department. "I'm Willa. Willa Tate. I actually already know you, or of you. I saw that news story they did last week. The one where you wore the tie. You know, the one with the stripes."

Kenneth knew the press conference. He also knew the tie.

He'd only expected her to bring up one of the two.

"You should have seen the Bugs Bunny tie I almost wore instead." It was a joke. And, boy, did Willa laugh. But there was a nervousness in it.

And then, like he'd flipped a switch, that laugh slid all the way down into the reason why she was there.

The heaviness became physical as she put her hand on top of the box that had seen much better days.

"A month ago I found this." Even her voice had hardened a little. No longer bright and chipper. She made no move to push the box over to him. "I unearthed it in a construction site and after seeing what was inside I… Well, I decided to take it home."

Despite himself, Kenneth leaned in a little closer.

"After everything that's happened with Kelby Creek and this department, I thought that maybe it was better to try to figure it out myself. Or, maybe get a clearer idea of what happened before I brought it in. But I've hit a dead end and I think it's time I ask for help."

"With what?" Kenneth pushed his pad of paper and pen to the side. The last round of locals he'd seen had sprouted instant conspiracy theories about dirty cops, bizarre and unlikely cold cases reaching back decades, and the ever-popular "I know what really happened to Annie McHale." None of the information had led anywhere other than to a cluster headache for Kenneth, but now he found himself intrigued.

Maybe because Willa Tate was herself intriguing.

She hesitated but answered with conviction.

"Solving a thirty-five-year-old murder."

Chapter Two

Detective Gray was a good *good*-looking man. Willa had almost forgotten her words and her thoughts when he'd sat across from her, slightly lost in her surprise.

Willa had seen the man before on the local news and in the paper more than once—it had been big news that a cold case unit was coming to the sheriff's department, even more so by a man who had returned to the job years after he'd left it behind. Then there was what had happened to his wife all those years ago that had made a news cycle or two in town. But there was just something about being close to him that changed her perspective from the man she'd never met but seen on TV.

He didn't much look like a small-town detective, lead of a task force or not. Instead he favored an actor playing the part of some big-time FBI agent in New York or Chicago. His brown hair was cut and groomed close and nice, just as his goatee beard made a controlled dusting of hair that took a good good-looking man and added some spice. His eyes were dark and blue and rested beneath thick eyebrows that expressed a seriousness she bet extended outside of work.

Then there was the jaw and the sun-kissed tan and the lean body and tall height, and Willa couldn't help but mentally stumble when he'd introduced himself.

But then, her reason for being there had come back and she'd pushed any and all attraction out the metaphorical window.

Now she watched as one of his eyebrows rose with concern and not physical interest.

"A thirty-five-year-old murder?" he repeated.

Willa kept her hand firmly on the box's lid. She nodded.

"I know it sounds out there, but yes, I think I got really close to figuring it out," she said. "Because of this."

Willa didn't want to slide the box over but knew it was the right thing to do. For some reason, she'd grown protective of it. Or, at least, some of its contents. She hadn't lied to the man, she'd squashed her first instinct to go to the sheriff's department when she'd found the box because she hadn't trusted that whatever was inside could be taken care of. So, she'd done some investigating on her own…and in the past month had become attached to a story she wasn't even sure was true.

Now it almost felt like giving the box over was her abandoning that hope.

Abandoning the woman in the photograph.

But you ran out of the story, she told herself. *It's time to get someone else to help you find the rest.*

Willa upped her smile in the hope that Detective Gray couldn't see the very real cracks beneath it. She carefully pushed the box across the table.

He took it when it was within reach.

Willa let out a small breath. It shook with relief, concern, and excitement.

Detective Gray's dark eyes met hers once more before focusing on the main reason for her being there. He was just as careful as he opened the container.

Willa knew exactly what he was seeing yet still listened with rapt attention as she listed off the contents.

"A ring box. A photograph of a young woman. One bullet casing…" He paused. Willa listed the last item currently in the box for him.

"A piece of ripped fabric. With what appears to be blood on it."

No matter his intensity or looks, Willa didn't like the skepticism that stretched across his face.

"Whose blood?"

Willa shook her head.

"I have no idea," she said. "I was hoping you'd be able to help me with that part."

Detective Gray took one last sweeping look across the box's contents. Then those dark eyes were on her. The skepticism still whirling around in them.

"And you found this at a construction site? How'd you know where to look?"

She'd been ready for this question but knew the answer sounded made up.

"A coworker had gone MIA and his wife called all concerned about him," Willa answered. "I offered to go look for him at the site he was working earlier that day. He wasn't there but I thought he might have dropped his phone. I found the box instead. Dave, the coworker, was fine by the way. He said he'd gotten wrapped up in a conversation with another worker about football. I suspect he got an earful when he got home, though."

There was a small stretch of silence as the detective scanned the items again. That skepticism stayed.

"I'm not saying that what's in this box isn't interesting," he started. "I'm just not sure how you think this pertains to a thirty-five-year-old murder. One that you want me to help you solve. If I'm being honest, this box actually looks like something for geocaching."

He must've realized she didn't know what that was. He tacked on an explanation.

"That's when you have a box in a certain location and you log those coordinates on a web site and then people go and look for it. Typically, when they find the box, they either write their name down on a list or take something out of the box before putting something back into the box." He waved his hand across the worn wood. "To me, that's what this looks like. An assortment of random objects. I mean these don't even look like they all come from the same time period. The picture looks like it was taken in the eighties. But this ring? It maybe looks a few years old."

Willa wasn't naïve enough to think that she would be believed the second she tried to explain. She knew that there were a whole lot of people in Kelby Creek who had been trying to knock down the door of the sheriff's department to see the new cold case unit. Her friend Ebony had been filling her in on some of the conspiracies and gossip that had been surrounding their fellow locals trying to get their piece of the newly developed unit and the former detective who had come back to be its leader.

Yet there was a sting in his words that cut into her. Willa wasn't used to not being trusted.

Even from a stranger.

She pushed her shoulders back, sat as tall as the chair would allow, and took great caution to keep her voice free of her swirling emotions starting up beneath the surface.

She also didn't want to betray the fact that, despite wanting the man to trust her, she was lying to him. At least, in part.

"At first, that's what I thought," she started. "That it was just random what was in there, but then I got lucky with the picture." Willa pointed to the box. The detective understood the motion. He pulled the picture out and glanced down at it before looking back to her as she continued. "That woman is Mae Linderman. I only was able to figure out who she was because, if you can see in the background of the picture, that's the old grocery store. I have a friend who works there now—you know, years after the remodel, of course. She was able to find out, through the owner and a lot of gossip, that Mae's brother worked there in the seventies. I was able to talk to him and, even though he was not a fan of discussing anything, he and the few people that I showed the picture to confirmed that that's Mae."

The detective nodded. Willa appreciated the gesture. At least it meant that he was paying attention and staying quiet long enough to let her tell the whole story.

"After I found out that it was, in fact, Mae, I learned that she passed away in '81 from a car accident."

The silence didn't last long.

"And you think it was murder? Something staged to look like an accident?"

"No," she replied a little too quickly. It was the first time Willa had said any of this to anyone. She hadn't told Ebony of her discovery or theory, and she hadn't told her sister Martha, either. It was exciting to tell someone finally. Exciting and frustrating. Especially when they were giving her a look like Detective Gray was giving her now.

"Once I learned about Mae, I learned about Josiah Linderman," she continued. "He was her husband and they married young. They had two kids and, despite the two of them working long hours, they didn't have much. They did, however, have each other and, from the few people I've talked to who actually knew them, their love was something else." Willa couldn't help but smile. She wasn't a stranger to love, falling into it with a partner or seeing it displayed by her family and friends, but a special love? True love? She didn't know if that was real. All she knew for sure was that she hadn't had it with Landon.

And if she hadn't had it with him, a man she'd been with for years, who was to say she would have it with anyone?

Across from her, the detective moved in his seat. It was subtle and… Maybe it was just a part of her imagination, but Willa thought the man had gone from scrutiny to discomfort. She kept on with the story and her theory so they wouldn't be bogged down in what was and instead find out what had happened after.

"A year after she died, Josiah said he was going to the store to get some groceries," she continued. "They lived in the house close to town limits, out near the creek. From his house to Main Street, it should've taken about ten minutes or so at a good pace to get there but Josiah'd been known to take the long way 'round to get to town. Instead of taking the paved roads, he detoured to the dirt ones that ran next to the woods, the creek, until finally he made it to Main. I mean, who doesn't prefer the long way around on a nice day? Especially us locals."

Detective Gray didn't comment, even when Willa had left him the space to do so if he wanted. She wasn't used to having a conversation so one-sided, even if she was explaining something. That might have had more to do with the fact that her sister could go a mile a minute when given the proper topic. Plus, as per her curse, Willa was trying to be polite.

She decided that this truly was the wrong place and the wrong time, so she finished the story without pausing again.

"Josiah never made it to the store and he never made it back home. According to Mae's brother, he just disappeared. A search party of friends was formed that night. They looked everywhere, but no one found a thing. He just was gone. Like snapping your fingers."

Willa motioned to the picture. "Like every town, there were, of course, people who said such bad things about him. A father consumed with grief overwhelmed at being a single parent leaves his kids to fall into foster care since they had no other family, apart from their uncle who refused to take them, and other such nasty things, but the few people I've talked to seemed to genuinely think the man cared about his kids. Even more so after his wife passed. He knew he was their only family. I don't think, at least from what I know about him, that Josiah would willingly abandon them."

Willa let her eyes wander to the photograph in the detective's hand. It was yellowing with age and there were worn marks from where it had been folded and unfolded many times.

"Though, to be honest, if it wasn't for that picture, I think I'd be inclined to believe that that box is just filled with random mess. Some scavenger hunt that maybe never got found. But rumor has it that ever since that picture was taken, Josiah had it on his person every moment except when he was sleeping.

"Whether it was in his pants' pocket, his wallet, or in his hand because he was showing someone his lovely wife, Josiah treasured that picture. So to find it in the box with a bullet casing and a bloodied piece of fabric? I don't think Josiah Linderman just disappeared. I think someone took him. And I think someone killed him, put the evidence in that box and buried it, hoping no one would ever find it. I think Josiah was murdered and I would very much like you to help me figure out by who."

There it was. The story Willa was trying to find.

The mystery she was trying to solve.

The one box that had consumed her thoughts since finding it buried at the construction site a month before.

And now she'd finally told someone.

And now it was time to see what Detective Gray thought.

EXPECTATIONS HAD A way of being a bit wild sometimes. What you thought you were going to get and what you actually got. It was like sitting there holding an empty cup while water poured into your hands instead.

In this situation, Kenneth felt like his cup was still waiting to catch some very vague conspiracy theory about the town or a neighbor. Instead he was sitting there holding a picture, a box, and a story about a man who left his family thirty-five years ago to go to the store.

And he didn't rightly know what to do with it at first.

Mainly because the one who had poured it all in had seemed more invested in finding out what had happened than in hoping for attention that many before her had come seeking.

Willa Tate gave off the impression that she very much wanted to help.

That was why he felt just a little regretful that he was going to have to shut her down.

"It's a shame what happened to that family," he said, using the voice he reserved for civilians when it came to the job. A voice he hadn't needed to use until recently. "But I'm not sure what I'm seeing here is a direct cause to believe in murder or to even prove that a man didn't just leave his family."

Willa opened her mouth. Ready, he assumed, to jump back into what she believed was the truth.

Maybe if Kenneth had lived a different life the last seven years or so, he would've let her. And Willa Tate could've tried to change his mind.

But Kenneth's life had been changed a while ago in the most violent of ways.

Every plan, every hope and every dream he'd ever had had been destroyed, rearranged, and painfully put to rest.

Along with a future he didn't recognize had come a perspective shift.

Before he'd been looking at the world with rose-colored glasses. Now he saw the world for what it was and his eyes continued to be bloodshot for it.

He hadn't come back to the sheriff's department, to a life in law enforcement, because he'd simply wanted to do good.

He'd come back because he'd wanted answers and justice, too.

And he couldn't have either if he accepted every far-fetched story that walked through the door. No matter how much she looked like sunshine.

"The best I can do for you right now, Miss Tate, is have you give me your number and I'll give you my card. I can look into the name to see if we have anything on file here." He powered on. "Though I have to warn you, since this unit was just formed, I'm the only one working through any of the files that come along with it until we can find someone else to hire who has the qualifications we're looking for. It might take a few days for me to find what's there or to see what's not. How about that?"

Kenneth didn't have to know the woman to under-stand that she was not a fan of anything he'd said.

"What about the bullet casing? What about the blood? Those aren't exactly things you typically find buried unless something's wrong. Right?"

"I'll admit, it is a bit odd, but I'm still not convinced it's not anything other than maybe geocaching or coin-cidence. I mean why bury the evidence to a murder and have it sit underground for that long when you can just destroy it some other way? The creek stretches far and wide here in town. There's a whole lot of forest, too. You could easily hide any one of these things between when Mr. Linderman went missing and now. Plus—" Kenneth pulled the smaller box out and turned it so she could see the ring. "I'm not at all an expert in jewelry, but I do believe this box comes from Cadence Jewel-ers in town, and they didn't open until 2002 or 2003. Why would it be in here with the rest of these items?"

Willa's sunshine had dimmed into what he could only describe as pointed determination. And it wasn't pointed at him.

"How do you know it's from Cadence Jewelers?" she asked. "The ring box, I mean."

For some reason Kenneth hadn't expected that ques-tion. He felt the tension in his body before he heard it in his voice.

"That trim on the inside is something the owner does specifically for locals. She calls it a nice personal touch. Also, most of the more prominent jewelers have a logo of some sort on theirs."

Kenneth didn't want to answer any more questions so

he stopped there, put the ring box back into the wooden one, and shut it. He was reaching for his business card as Willa pulled the box back to her.

"I'll let you know if I find anything," he said, passing it over as he stood.

Rising, Willa Tate produced her own card. Clanton Construction was typed in fine print across the top.

"Thank you." Her voice was clipped but she didn't continue.

Kenneth walked her to the door. It was only when she was through the threshold that she stopped and turned back to look at him.

"This town has had a habit of losing people, whether it be through some violent means or just by falling through the cracks." Her eyes narrowed on him. Her nostrils flared. If he had the time, Kenneth believed he could have counted every freckle across her face given how close they were. Instead he got the sharp end of good intentions and extreme determination. "Josiah Linderman may be gone but I will not let his memory and what happened to him fall through the cracks. And you shouldn't, either."

The contents of the box shifted as Willa turned on her heel and walked herself back out to the lobby.

Kenneth could have almost sworn that the hallway became a little darker in her wake.

Chapter Three

Martha could tell something was wrong. She'd been like that for as long as Willa could remember. It didn't matter if it had something to do with a bad day at school, a crush who didn't like her back, or client interaction that rubbed her the wrong way, Martha Tate-Smith had a knack for knowing when to bring the sweet tea and cookies to her sister.

"Willa Tate, I know you're in there," her sister could be heard calling at the side door at the top of the stairs next to the garage. "Not only is your car parked out here but I saw you walking like a bee was in your britches. Now open up so we can talk about it while we take in our God-given daily dose of sugar that we don't need."

Willa thought about not opening the door. Sure, technically Martha was her landlord and, sure, she was her sister. But Willa was so mad that she knew seeing Martha, cookies or not, wouldn't make that bee in her britches go away.

When Willa had gone to the sheriff's department, she'd hoped to find someone who at the very least would listen and at the very most take action. Find whatever information they could about Josiah Linderman and maybe come up with a plan for next steps. Instead she'd been given a card with a number, a vague outline of what was next, and a warning that nothing might be found or done.

It hadn't been an inspiring meeting, which was a feeling that had rolled over into uninspiring frustration an hour later.

A frustration that she was going to have a hard time hiding from her sister.

Willa took the wooden box and placed it in its hiding spot. She let out a sigh and went to the door.

"Aren't you supposed to be at work?" Willa asked in greeting when the door was open.

While Willa was big blond hair and freckles, Martha was smooth dark hair and one singular mole on her right cheek. The difference between them was all down to genetics. Willa had taken after her mother and Martha had taken after their father. But personality wise? Both sisters had somehow become more like each other than anyone else.

That was why living with each other could be disastrous on any given day.

"Don't you go sassing me," Martha shot back. She pushed inside the apartment, the smell of cookies wafting off of the plate as she passed. "I'm just here to make sure you're okay. First you say you're taking off work for a personal day and then you come back here looking all scrunched face and bothered? You better believe that I'm going to come ask what's going on."

Willa followed her sister to the kitchenette in the corner.

Despite it being above the garage, the mother-in-law suite was surprisingly spacious. The living area, including the kitchenette, was big enough for a couch, a TV, a desk and four barstools at the counter. Two of those barstools were occupied by indoor plants that, for whatever reason, Willa couldn't seem to keep alive. Martha's husband, Kimball, liked to joke those were the stools where houseplants went to die. Past them and through the doorway next to the small refrigerator was the bedroom. It was smaller but had everything Willa might need.

Though even if it had been lacking, it was still better than living with Landon right after they'd broken up. Willa liked to be an optimist, but even that situation had caused her a few stomachaches of worry before Martha had stepped in.

"I took a personal day to do a few personal things," Willa responded, taking a seat next to her currently dying plant. "That means it's none of your business unless I say so. Okay?"

Martha rolled her eyes as she took the Saran wrap off the plate. She worked part-time at a bakery downtown. Her specialty was chocolate chip and peanut butter cookies. But it was her Oreo cheesecake that was her absolute gift to mankind. That was why both Willa and Martha's husband had made a rule that she wasn't allowed to bring that specific work home with her.

"Willa, if you're using that 'it's none of my business' line on me then it has to be about a boy," Martha concluded with quickness. "Last time, it looked like you sucked the end of a lemon when we were talking about the guy you dated—what's his name? The one with the tattoos?"

Willa had to chuckle at that.

"Are you talking about Rodney? Rodney Bishop?"

Martha did a small clap. "Bingo!"

"First of all, I didn't date Rodney," Willa corrected. "I went on a date with him after Landon, and while it wasn't bad, it was better for all involved to just stay friends. Second, every time I'm frustrated doesn't mean it's about a man. I think that could be considered sexist, you know?"

Martha took a cookie and went to the fridge to pull out the jug of sweet tea. She started pouring her glass while talking around the bite of cookie in her mouth.

"Well, it's not like you're exactly out here living some kind of exciting life. No offense—"

"Hey! Much offense," Willa interrupted.

Martha kept on like she hadn't said a word. "—so excuse me for assuming it had something to do with relationships. But if it isn't about some man," she continued, "then what is it about? Did something happen at work?"

Willa might have been older by two years, but there were moments when concern for her family overtook Martha that she seemed older and—dare Willa think it?—maternal. She finished pouring her tea and leaned against the counter, nearly matching eyes on Willa.

"You can talk to me, you know?" Martha added. "I won't judge."

Willa wasn't worried about her sister judging her for what she had done the last month. She didn't think

Martha would give her any grief over the fact that, for almost four weeks, she had doubled down on a mystery that may or may not exist. That her heart was starting to—or maybe, as she suspected, already had—become attached to a man and his family who had been gone for thirty-five years. Willa should have told her sister then, between the dying plant and fresh cup of sweet tea, all about the box and its collection of odd contents.

But then she thought of what wasn't in the box any-more.

The one item she had taken out and hidden in a sep-arate place.

The one object that might have piqued Detective Gray's attention, despite his reservations about Willa's story.

She might have trusted her sister, respected and loved her, but something about what had happened to Josiah and the box kept Willa's stomach tight.

She didn't want to tell Martha because it felt like any-one else knowing would put them in danger somehow. Just like when someone can feel someone else staring at them or watching them. It was a simple feeling that Willa couldn't escape.

Though it was one she was hoping would have gone away had Detective Gray believed her.

"I know I can talk to you," Willa said, voice soft. "But I'm fine. Today's personal day was work-related and frustrating, but nothing bad. I'm just tired. I didn't sleep that well last night."

It wasn't all a lie but it wasn't all the truth. Guilt and

shame pushed frustration and anger out of Willa but she stuck with what she'd said. She didn't know what was worse, though. The fact that Martha seemed to believe her or the fact it was so easy to let her believe her. Either way, the subject changed, they ate cookies together and, after a while Martha declared it was time to go back to work.

She patted the top of Willa's hand before she left.

"Don't forget family dinner will be this week," Martha said halfway out the door. "I cooked last week so you and Kimball are combining your powers to make this meal."

"Oh, I won't forget," Willa assured her sister. "Mom's already promised to send me a recipe to attempt."

Martha laughed. "God help us all!"

Willa would have taken offense to that but it was like another switch had flipped within her. Talk of a normal family dinner made her think about Josiah. Thinking about Josiah made her think of the box. And thinking about the box?

Well, that led her to the small window seat at the front of the room.

Willa looked around as if someone had somehow snuck in and was hiding in the room with her. She waited a few moments and then pulled up on the cushion.

There was no box inside. Or at least not a sturdy one.

She took the lid off of a shoebox and stared at what she should have told the detective about.

A shiver went up her spine.

Willa had never been comfortable around guns.

THE DAY DRAGGED out longer than Kenneth's sinus med-ication supply lasted. By the time five o'clock rolled around, his head felt like it was trapped in a vise.

"You know, Delilah, there are some people up north who don't even know what humidity is. One day you and I are going to pack our things, take a truck, and just head north. What do you think about that?"

Delilah didn't seem to mind the fantasy. She wagged her tail and then let out a yawn. Kenneth gave her a gentle pat. Despite the building pressure in his head, he smiled. There was just something about a dog that made the world a little bit better.

A rap against the door made that tail wagging go into overdrive.

He turned to see Foster Lovett filling his doorframe. Lovett was the lead detective for the sheriff's depart-ment and one of the reasons why Kenneth had agreed to return. For all the hot water the department had found itself in with the town a few years prior, Lovett had been doing his damnedest to pull them all out of the mud. He'd also, according to the sheriff, been the reason why the cold case unit had been formed. Getting each case solved and sorted wasn't just a job to Lovett; it was more important. And that had gained Kenneth's respect.

He also had seen Delilah earlier and had only smiled, polite.

That, too, made Kenneth like him more.

"Hey there, Lovett. How can I help you?"

The detective leaned in the doorway. There was a file beneath his arm and he was rubbing his wedding band with his thumb. He looked tired but Kenneth didn't know if that was from work or the newborn baby he and his wife, Millie, had at home.

"I just came in here to check on you," he responded with a smile. "I saw how crowded the lobby got today. If I hadn't been on the way to court to testify in a case, I might have given you a hand to help cut down on how many people you had to talk to."

Kenneth shrugged. "This is the job," he said simply. "Everyone thinks they have a story and it's my duty to listen to the stories… Even if it makes me want to drink more coffee than I'm sure is good for me."

Both men laughed. Most of the people in the department had a running joke about how much coffee each of them drank, especially since the county coroner, Amanda Alvarez, had come to the department to school them all on their health.

"You can't help people if you don't help yourself," she'd said. "Make some healthy choices. For starters, maybe don't drink your weight in coffee before noon every day."

No one had promised her they would cut down on their coffee yet Kenneth had been surprised to see that some had actually followed her advice, most notably Deputy Park. Though that might have less to do with his personal health and more to do with the fact that he seemed to be a big fan of Dr. Alvarez. But that wasn't Kenneth's business.

"Well, either way, I'm impressed that you made it through them all," Foster continued. "Did anyone tell you anything you think has actionable information?"

Kenneth ran his hand through his hair, using the

small gesture to buy him an extra second or two to think about how he wanted to respond.

"There were a few people who gave me names and spoke about cases they believed had been filed wrong. Most of them I already knew about. Just like I knew most of the people who brought it up were directly involved with those who, because of whatever crime they'd committed, are now serving time. Still, I'll look into them, but I don't imagine we'll get anything new there. Also, there was another name I was given that I hadn't heard before."

"Oh yeah? Who?"

"Josiah Linderman?"

Lovett's eyebrows came together in contemplation. "Linderman... I can't say that rings a bell. Who is he?"

"Some man who disappeared thirty-five years ago around here. There allegedly was no proof of foul play and many thought he'd left town of his own accord. Now I have a woman who believes he was murdered instead. Thinks she found some evidence that points to her conclusion."

"Hmm. If I recognized the name, I could throw in my two cents, but even if I hadn't left town for over a decade before coming back, I'd say that's a little bit before my time. But you know Sheriff Chamblin was here then. If you think there's some credence to the story, I'd go talk to him tomorrow. He should be in-house for at least the morning before having to deal with more of the press." Lovett smiled. It was a humoring one.

Kenneth might not have worked previously under Sheriff Chamblin but he knew enough about the older man to know that talking to the press was his least favorite thing to do when it came to his duties. He also wasn't big on sitting behind the desk, yet that's what he'd been doing more and more lately. Though, after what had happened to Annie McHale, being transparent with the community and making damn sure the department was completely aboveboard might have been the most boring aspect of his job, it was now one of the most important.

Still, that didn't mean the sheriff had to like it. He might actually welcome the change of talking about a potential cold case.

"All right," Kenneth said. "I'll talk to him tomorrow to see if he knows anything."

"Sounds good to me. Are you about to head out?"

Kenneth nodded and rolled his chair back. He already had Delilah's leash in his hand. "If I don't get her home and take her for a walk, I'm sure there'll be hell to pay later on when I'm trying to fall asleep."

Lovett laughed again.

"Same goes for me and not relieving Millie from Mom duty soon," he said. "She loves our son a whole lot but you should see her pass him off like a football as soon as I make it to the property line. Not that I blame her. I don't think she's slept since he was born."

It was meant as a way to end the conversation on a casual note. Something polite to say instead of just saying "Okay, I'm headed out because it's the end of my shift." But it struck a chord that often got played when people around Kenneth spoke of their families.

No matter how many years went by, there were some moments that reminded him of his own lost family.

Of Ally's death.

Of her murder.

Of a man in a mask who had, for no reason that anyone knew of, decided to kill her while she'd been out for a jog.

Kenneth balled his fist, the leash in his grip and pen in the other hand.

He glanced down at the top of his desk and at the pad of paper he'd been writing on that day.

There were names and cases that filled the small page.

Yet there was one name that Kenneth eyed with ease among the others.

Josiah Linderman.

Chapter Four

The sheriff had been surprisingly absent the next day.

So Kenneth spent that Tuesday night sitting on his back porch, in a patio chair that had seen much better days, and watching Delilah run around.

All the while thinking about freckles and sunshine. About how something nagged at him about Willa Tate.

Kenneth had intended to talk to the sheriff today about Josiah, but when it had become clear that talk was going to have to wait, he'd dug into the files in his office, searching for any hard-copy records of cases from 1984 through 1986. Surprisingly there weren't many cases that had been challenging or unsolved from the timeframe. A robbery turned deadly. A bike theft. A complaint of harassment by an anonymous source against a man who'd owned the hardware store in town at the time.

In most small towns that would be normal—the whole "not having a lot of cases that piqued much interest"—but Kelby Creek wasn't normal. It hadn't been for years.

Delilah barked and then shot across the yard to the

corner of the fence. Just as quickly as her attention had diverted to it, it switched again to the other side of the yard. She bounded playfully, just enjoying being outside. Kenneth imagined she was mostly happy to no longer be sitting in his dusty office. She was free here. At least, free from all the violence and wrongdoing that surround them both in the storage room at the department.

Kenneth reached for the beer that he had opened an hour ago. It was no longer cold but it was completely full. He rubbed his thumb along the label and snorted as a memory floated through.

I've never met a man who has such a hard time learning to relax. If bad guys can sit back and drink beer, and not worry about the law like you catching them, then I think you can enjoy a drink every now and then, too.

Kenneth hadn't heard Ally's voice in almost eight years. And that was only because, on the anniversary of her death, he'd finally mustered up the courage to listen to a voice mail he'd been diligently saving. The last one she'd left him. But sitting here now, it was like she was standing at his ear and repeating something she had often told him throughout their marriage.

"I know how to relax," he would always say, trying to defend himself.

"Whatever you say."

Ally's lips would then turn up at the corners and she would smile a brief, beautiful smile, and Kenneth would slowly start to relax. She'd always been good at that. While he was in his own head about work, about cases, she'd remind him that there was more than just what was in his head.

Kenneth put the beer bottle back down.

He looked at his cell phone and then at the card lying against the thigh of his jeans. Willa Tate's name was in bold.

After he'd gotten home last night, he had done a social media search of the woman. Mostly to see if she was the kind of person who posted all over the internet about wild, outlandish things but partially because he was curious. Kenneth had grown up in Kelby Creek but he'd spent his summers in Georgia at his grandparents' home. After he'd graduated high school, he'd moved there for a few years to go to school for criminology. Then he'd gone to the academy and right back to Kelby Creek, accepting a job as a deputy.

In his absences, he'd missed a few new faces, forgotten some old ones, and had run into several he'd wished he'd never see again. Small towns were like that. At least, he felt that way. You couldn't go to the grocery store without running into at least three people you knew, but you could go to a football game and stare into the crowd and not know at least twenty of the people staring back.

That's who Willa Tate was to him. A local in the crowd he'd just managed to never meet.

According to the internet and her public posts, she was a few years younger than him, seemed to like to laugh a lot, and was surprisingly single.

The last detail shouldn't have mattered but he found himself making a note of it anyway. A small piece of information that held no bearing whatsoever on her interest in Josiah Linderman and the box she'd brought to the department. Yet he'd wondered why a person who was like sunshine didn't have someone in her life bathing in her light. It seemed a damn shame, if he was being honest.

Apart from those small facts that he gleaned off the internet, Willa seemed like a normal woman. And by normal, he meant not the type who would try to dig up someone else's tragic past for attention or any kind of fame.

That was why he was on his back porch this Tuesday night in the first place. Watching his dog run and play, his mind coming back to Josiah Linderman, the box and the nagging feeling that he'd missed something during his conversation with Willa Tate yesterday at the department.

It took him another hour or so to realize that what he was feeling had less to do with what she'd said and more to do with what she hadn't. Also, the box itself. If it did contain the clues to an unsolved murder, why put them in a box so big? It was almost like something was missing, and that bothered him.

It bothered him as he lay awake in bed later that night. It continued to bother him on Wednesday morning as he drank his coffee and took Delilah out for one last walk. As he talked to his neighbor and thanked her for keeping an eye on his golden pooch while he was at work. And all the way to his office with the Storage placard on the door.

So he grabbed his pad of paper, pen and coffee

thermos, and marched down the hall to the door that read Sheriff.

He knocked and was glad to hear a callout in response.

"Come in!"

Kenneth opened the door to reveal a burly man with laugh lines, gray hair, and a cowboy hat on the desktop. He had a folder open in front of him with a stack of papers on top. He didn't look displeased to see Kenneth, but it wasn't hard to tell that, if given the choice to teleport to some faraway tropical island versus continue to do whatever paperwork he was looking at, he'd be on some sandy beach drinking mai tais.

"Hey, boss. If you didn't mind, I was wondering if we could talk for second?"

Interim Sheriff Brutus Chamblin dropped the pen like it was a snake ready to bite him.

"No offense, Gray, but talking to a wall right now would be preferable to doing this paperwork." He shook his head. "You know there were days during retirement where I'd get so antsy that I felt like I was about to run out of my skin. Now that I'm back until this town can get a new sheriff I think about fishing with an ice-cold beer in one hand and my no-good brother-in-law complaining about being too hot at my shoulder, and I'll be a daggum monkey's uncle if I don't miss it something fierce."

Kenneth laughed. "Everyone's got something to say about working, but no one really tells you what to do with retirement. Though I do think that's the point."

Chamblin chuckled then shrugged. "Well, if that ain't the truth."

His posture went from casual to a little more stiff. The humor that planted the crinkles at the edges of his eyes was gone. In its place was a man who was good at his job and wanted others to be good at theirs, too. "Now, what brings you here to me before you've even finished your first cup of coffee?"

"I met with a woman two days ago who claims that she might have information on an unsolved murder back in the eighties. The murder of a Josiah Linderman. I looked through the files, but couldn't find anything on him, not even a missing persons report, so I was wondering if you knew Josiah or knew of him?"

Chamblin took a moment to think. Then he nodded.

"It's been a while since I heard the name but, yeah, I knew Josiah. Well, I'd gone to church with him and his wife before she passed. We'd said a few words here and there but weren't close. Let's see... When he went missing, I would have been a deputy here. Not on the job too long. I can't speak to anyone filing or not filing a missing persons report, but I do remember helping our church along with others to look for him."

"And you didn't find anything," Kenneth suggested.

Chamblin shook his head.

"One Sunday he was there and the next there was an empty seat in one of the pews. After a while, the name and what happened just kind of faded. Sad to say it but true." His eyebrow rose, even more curious than Kenneth had been when Willa had first told him her theory. "This woman, did she find a body?"

It was Kenneth's turn to shake his head.

"No, sir. But she thinks she's found enough for me to look into. Before I made my decision, I wanted to see what you knew."

"I'm afraid that's all I have. It was a long time ago and, as much as I like to say my memory is a steel trap, just as it had been when I was a deputy or a detective, I'd be lying." He gave Kenneth a small but genuine smile. "I trust your judgment on this. That's the whole reason why you are the only man we had fingered for the cold case unit. You've got good instincts and a drive that a lot of people just don't have. Let me know what you decide."

Kenneth, ready to leave after he'd said a quick thank you, paused before he made it to the door.

"You know, throughout my career, at least up until this point, I've noticed that when people say someone has 'disappeared,' it's because they can't decide if that person left of their own free will or was forced. Now, if it's clear the person didn't leave of their own volition, they usually say 'taken.' And then there are people who use the word 'missing.' In my experience that typically means they've made up their mind and believe the person in question didn't just run off, that something happened to them. Something most likely that was bad."

The sheriff's brow furrowed for a moment. "I'm guessing I said 'missing,' didn't I?"

Kenneth nodded. "Yes, you did. You think Josiah Linderman was killed, don't you?"

Chamblin sighed. "I guess I do, despite there not being a lick of evidence to support the idea."

"Can I ask why?"

The sheriff didn't have to think on it this time.

"Grief or not, he loved his kids. You didn't have to know him that well to see that they meant the world to him. I don't think there's any way he would've let them willingly go into the system. He was all they had."

It wasn't a fancy answer, but it didn't have to be fancy to be a good one.

"Thanks, Sheriff. I'll let you know if anything progresses on this."

Kenneth went back to his office. He had to take care of a few things and then make a call.

IT WAS THE big boss's birthday and after lunch everyone went home. Well, everyone was told they could go home but instead the party continued on at the only bar in Kelby Creek.

The Rosewater Inn was a smattering of weird decisions.

In the first stage of its life, it had been a motel. In the second stage, it had been partially renovated to a bed-and-breakfast. When that hadn't gone anywhere, the next life stage took an even stranger turn, and the Rosewater was divided into three pieces. To the left, when standing in the parking lot facing the building, there was the portion that had been made into the bar. The middle section, transformed into storage, had been closed off to everyone but the owners for the last several years. The right portion of the building had been converted into rental office suites. At the moment, there was a salon, an accountant and a bona fide psychic—according to her sign in the window.

All in all, the Rosewater was just one of those places that was definitely unique.

It was also a place where you could find trouble if you had too many of their specialty drinks. Last time Willa had gone with Ebony after work she'd sent a text to one of her exes saying that she still wanted to kiss his face, somehow lost a shoe, and had woken up with one the worst hangovers she'd had since college. So when the party went from celebrating her boss turning seventy with cake, soda and a sandwich platter to being at the Rosewater at 2:00 p.m. on a Wednesday with a bunch of construction workers grateful for paid break, Willa made sure to enjoy herself while staying on her best behavior.

Though that plan wobbled its way out the door when her phone rang. The Caller ID read Unknown. She excused herself from Ebony's side to go out to the parking lot to take the call.

"Hello?"

Before the voice came through the line Willa had hoped it would be Detective Gray on the other end but when she actually heard his voice, her stomach still fluttered.

"Miss Tate? This is Detective Gray, with the Dawn County Sheriff's Department. We met on Monday."

"Oh, hi, Detective! What can I do you for? Did you find anything about Josiah?"

There was no hesitation on the other side of the phone.

"No, but I would like to meet with you again. Today,

if possible. Would you mind if I swung by your work? I'm out of the office on some business and thought it would be easier."

Willa had a rule about not letting anyone make her feel embarrassed unless she'd earned it, but the heat of a blush was making its way up her neck and into her cheeks. Unfortunately, there was no way around where she currently was.

A bar.

On a Wednesday afternoon.

Not exactly normal operating hours.

Also not something she wanted being spread as gossip around the department if he repeated the information.

"I… I'm not at work right now. How about meeting at the coffee shop on Main? I can be there in twenty?"

Detective Gray wasn't as quick to respond, but after a moment she felt like he nodded into his answer of okay.

"I'll see you there in twenty, Miss Tate."

Chapter Five

Half an hour went by. Then another ten minutes. Before another five could pass, Kenneth gave Willa another call.

Her phone rang and rang and rang.

Then her voice mail played with her telling whoever was calling that she must have stepped away from her phone, to leave a name, number and reason for their call, and she would call them back. It was a professional message yet... There was a tone of happiness he assumed was her natural state as she said to have a good day at the end of it.

This time Kenneth left a message.

"Hey there, Miss Tate. This is Detective Gray again. I'm at the café and got a little curious as to where you might be. Give me a call back. I hope to see you soon."

Another few minutes went by and there was no Willa Tate to be seen.

Kenneth paid for his coffee, asked the barista if Willa came in to tell her to call him, and tried to walk around the feeling in his gut he was not liking at all.

He pulled her business card back out as soon as he

settled behind the wheel of his SUV. This time he called Clanton Construction's main number printed beneath hers.

After a few rings, a man picked up. It was clear that, based on the noise in the background, the man was probably not at a construction site.

"This is Bobby. How can I help you this fine, fine afternoon?" There was laughter in the background along with a lot of chatter. Whoever Bobby was, he also sounded like he was having a good time.

"Hi there, Bobby. I was actually looking for Willa Tate? Is this where I can reach her?"

The sound of movement made the connection go slightly static. Wherever Bobby was, he hadn't left the commotion, though Kenneth guessed he'd stepped away from it enough to hear better.

"We actually closed early today due to an office event."

"Then Willa is with you?"

Maybe she was with her coworkers and had just lost track of time?

"Uh, can I ask who's asking for her?" Bobby's voice went from fun to focused in an instant.

Kenneth assumed he was friends with Willa, so he got to the point without giving away the reason.

"My name's Kenneth. I am an acquaintance of Willa's. We had plans to meet for coffee and she hasn't showed up, so I was wondering where she is."

The sound of movement was loud again in Kenneth's ear. Bobby called out to somebody. That person answered, but Kenneth couldn't hear what was said. It didn't matter. He realized he already knew that Willa wasn't there. But he waited for Bobby to confirm.

"Sorry, she left maybe a half hour ago. I can take a message for her if you want to leave one, though."

Kenneth didn't want to leave a message. What he did want was information. After very little questioning, he found out that most of Clanton Construction was at the Rosewater Inn. He kept his thoughts to himself as to why they were at a bar so early in the day and ended the call.

Putting his SUV in gear, he drove a little faster than he should have to the only bar in town.

It was nothing, he told himself.

Willa had just gotten sidetracked somewhere between the bar and the café.

Two days after she had brought a potential unsolved murder to him and the same afternoon that he just so happened to want to meet her and talk about it.

It was a coincidence that the woman he'd met who was so gung-ho about finding justice was now gone and not answering her phone.

Even as he thought it, Kenneth gripped the steering wheel with force.

Willa was probably fine. But he couldn't shake the growing sense of urgency.

So, a few minutes out from the bar, he decided to use his SUV's hands-free calling to try the woman's cell one more time.

He could be overreacting, the feeling in his gut there because Kelby Creek had a history of people just disappearing.

A history of phone calls being made but never answered.

Of women there one day and gone the next.

Kenneth tried to shake the thoughts that were starting to trail somewhere dark. Somewhere he never wanted to go again.

But then the phone stopped ringing and Willa answered.

Though, judging by the fact she answered in a whisper, he assumed it wasn't time to feel relief just yet.

"Detective Gray?" Her voice was low and hurried.

Kenneth slowed his speed, ready to turn off the road to give her his full attention if needed.

"Willa? What's wrong?"

The woman didn't immediately answer. Much like her coworker Bobby, the sound of movement traveled across the line. However, unlike Bobby, Kenneth couldn't hear any type of chatter or commotion in the background. Instead there was her movement and then silence.

Kenneth eyed the console screen for second to see if the call had ended but then Willa's voice came through again.

"I'm at my apartment, above my sister's garage," she said, so low he almost couldn't hear her.

Kenneth matched her volume. Something was wrong. There was panic and fear in her voice even if it was faint.

"What's going on?"

When she answered, it was like a whisper on the wind.

Something that passed you by and left nothing in its wake.

"Someone else is here."

Adrenaline surged through him at her words. He was grateful in that moment for a memory that was mostly good. Thanks to his internet search the day before, he'd confirmed that she was in fact a local and had noted her last listed address.

He started to turn the SUV around, knowing exactly where he needed to head next.

"Who is with you?" There was no answer. "Willa?" He made sure to keep his voice as quiet as possible. "Willa? Are you there?"

She didn't answer.

The phone call ended.

EBONY HAD ONCE told Willa a story about how she was taking yoga to help spice things up in the bedroom with her husband. When Willa, who had been in the middle of filing at work at the time, had asked why, her friend had laughed.

"It's all about being flexible," Ebony had responded. "When you're flexible and bendy, you can have more *fun*."

Ebony had wiggled her eyebrows after she'd said it, which had only made Willa laugh all the more.

"And here I thought people did yoga for health benefits and strength."

They'd shared another laugh when Ebony had pointed out that being bendy was a benefit to everyone involved before Willa had admitted that she was as flexible as a straight arrow.

"Sounds like you should do some yoga then," Ebony

had responded. "You never know how important it is to be flexible until you're in a situation where you want to be."

Willa had waved the woman off when she'd said it because they both knew the situation she was talking about was one in the bedroom behind closed doors and beneath the sheets.

But now?

Now Willa wished that she was a bendy, flexible person.

If she managed to get out of her hiding place, she swore to herself that she would take Ebony up on the offer of joining her at yoga.

That was if whoever was ransacking her apartment didn't find her first.

Because as much as she was okay with the size of her living space on any given day, the truth was that it was small. Thus, it would only be a matter of time before the man riffling through her things got to the window seat and, since the cushion that normally rested on top was no longer there, be able to see the seat's hinges and know that it opened.

And that an un-bendy, nonflexible woman was hiding inside trying to be as quiet as possible.

Footsteps sounded somewhere near the counter at the kitchenette. Something scraped the floor; the intruder must have moved a stool that had already fallen when he'd first entered. Willa didn't have time to replay all the ways she could've handled herself better when her uninvited guest had started trying to break through her door. It wasn't like there were many places to hide or a way to escape. She could have jumped from the second floor onto the concrete below to the driveway or tried to find a weapon. She could have done a lot of other things probably a lot smarter than smooshing herself into the window seat.

But she hadn't.

The only thing she had done that had made a lick of sense was to grab her cell phone.

Shortly after, Detective Gray had started to call. She'd been quick to put her phone on silent. Willa had wanted to answer the first two calls but instead she watched the phone light up the board beneath her. She couldn't tell exactly where her intruder was but then she heard him moving around her desk. At that point she'd been too afraid to move. Too afraid to even dial 9-1-1.

She also couldn't remember if the keys on her phone made noise as you typed in a number.

Then she couldn't remember the emergency setup on her phone. Wasn't there just one button to push? One key to alert the authorities without making a noise?

Her heart had been and was still beating a mile a minute.

When the detective called for a third time, Willa found some luck.

She heard the intruder rummaging around in her bedroom. Plenty of distance between the two of them where, if she talked quietly enough, the outsider couldn't hear her.

Then her luck, as small as it was, disappeared.

The footsteps returned to the living area and she ended the call.

Those footsteps came closer to her hiding place.

Willa held her breath.

Just go away, she silently pleaded.

She should have just gone straight to the coffee shop from the bar. She shouldn't have come home to change into something nicer. Why had it mattered what she'd been wearing?

Because you wanted to make a good second impression. Because, even though he ticked you off by not believing you, he looked darn good doing it. That's why you're wearing a sundress and not your work slacks. That's also why there's a tube of lipstick on the counter that you dropped before your bad mistake was banging through the door.

Willa berating herself was a good distraction for the moment.

Her heart didn't beat as fast and she wasn't on the brink of crying anymore.

She was just waiting.

Waiting for a man she didn't know to hopefully find her address, speed her way, and save the day from the intruder taking his dear sweet time to rob her.

Because that's surely what he was doing, right?

Those footsteps sounded like gunshots now. They were closer. There was nothing in the world that could take Willa's mind or nerves off of the fact that whoever was standing next to her hiding place was either looking out the window or looking down at the lid of the seat.

She should have just worn her slacks.

The intruder grabbed the lid of the window seat and started to pull up. The creak from the hinges that needed oiling were squeaking before the guy could even get his fingers beneath the lip.

Ice went through Willa's veins.

And sirens sounded in the distance.

Police sirens.

It was enough to change the next order of events.

As the lid rose, Willa pushed up with her back and aching, partially numbed legs, and yelled something awful.

She didn't have time to take in the details of the intruder shocked by her sudden presence. All she could catalog before she went into fight-or-flight mode was that it was a man. He was wearing a mask and an oversize jacket, and he was much, much bigger than she was.

"Help! *Help!*"

Willa's momentum and now raging adrenaline and fear toppled over the side of the wooden seat she had just sprung up from. The man, still coming to terms with her appearance, had stumbled a foot or so back. Her yelling for help seemed to shake him out of his surprise. He went for her as she hit the ground, palms first, elbows second, knees third.

His hands, large meaty things encased in gloves, planted themselves on either side of her rib cage and pulled up. It was an awkward and off-putting thing for him to do, driving his momentum down at an odd angle while she tried to roll out of his hold.

Soon both of them were on the floor.

"Help!" she yelled again, struggling with her voice.

Willa managed to flip onto her back in time to use

her arms and legs to try to keep the man from grabbing at her again.

For a large man, he was deceptively fast.

He was on his feet and using one of them in a flash.
His boot pushed Willa's flailing leg closest to him to the
ground. She cried out in pain and then in absolute fear
as he used one of his hands to grab her wrist. He pinned
the right side of her body to her own living-room floor.

"Let…let me *go*!"

The man didn't relent. Willa tried to get out of his
hold and move her leg at the same time. He held fast to
his position. When Willa tried to use her left hand to
free the other, he was unfazed. It was like hitting and
clawing at a wall.

"The cops—the cops are coming," she croaked.

Willa prayed that the sirens they heard were actually
heading to her location, but just as she had the thought,
their volume decreased. They were heading away from
them. It was a cruel twist of fate. One that the intruder
must have found joy in.

He didn't speak but he did chuckle.

Every part of Willa deflated at the sound.

Tears started to prick the corners of her eyes.

She thought of her sister and her parents and her
friends.

She thought of Josiah Linderman. Wondered if she,
too, was about to go missing as she was convinced he had.

The intruder used his free hand and slipped it into
his jacket pocket.

Willa started to fight again; a fish pulled from the
creek water and struggling to get back.

He had expected that. Whatever was in his pocket, he didn't pull it out.

Instead, he did something that might've been even more terrifying.

He removed his foot from Willa's thigh and dropped to his knee next to her on the floor. Before she could do anything, his right hand went around her neck.

Willa tried to scream but he snuffed out the sound.

Blinded by fear and panic and pain, she was convinced she was about to die.

Chapter Six

Kenneth was seeing red.

Red and black and sunshine yellow.

The only thought that went through his head was not to shoot for fear of hitting Willa. Instead he did what he believed anyone else would do.

Kenneth was on the man the second he stepped through the door of Willa's apartment.

The punch caught the man wearing black off guard, but not as much as the tackle. The attacker might have been tall and wide but so was he. And if a career in law enforcement had taught Kenneth anything, it was that a person with surprise on their side often had the best advantage.

They both fell backward onto the floor though Kenneth managed to get to his feet much faster. He threw another punch with every intention of trying to knock the man out.

It didn't take.

Instead, Kenneth took an uppercut that nearly put him back on the floor.

Behind him, Willa could be heard coughing.

Then the red returned.

The anger.

The rage.

The absolute audacity of the man for attacking a woman in her home.

Of trying to strangle her.

All while wearing a mask.

The past rushed into his heart just as Kenneth's gut told him what to do in the present.

He felt that anger and rage vibrate through him, riding along with his adrenaline. This time when his fist connected with the man beneath him, he knew it was going to end their fight.

The man grunted but didn't swing out again.

Kenneth took a step back and pulled out his service weapon again. He'd placed it back in its holster when he'd realized he couldn't get a clear hit on the man without endangering Willa when he'd first come into the apartment.

Yet, the man was fast. He had his own gun in hand in a second flat.

Kenneth should fire off a shot.

But there was Willa to consider.

He didn't know exactly where she was behind him and he didn't know if he could shield her if the man got a shot off first.

"Let's keep calm," he said. "This doesn't need to escalate. I'm with the Dawn County Sheriff's Department. We can figure this out without anyone else getting hurt."

By the widening of his eyes, the only thing Kenneth could see through the ski mask was that the news carried some kind of weight. The man stood slowly, gun trained on Kenneth, but the aggression that had been pouring off the man in waves had lessened.

When his eyes darted to the door, he was forced to do the one thing Kenneth assumed he'd been trying not to.

He spoke.

"I'm a fast shot." His voice was deep, gravel-filled. It was also strained. He was hurting. "You might be able to stop me but not before I can kill her. Let me leave and I won't."

"I can't just let you leave," Kenneth said.

"Then you're about to be in a room with two dead bodies."

Willa made a noise.

Kenneth had to admit the statement was chilling.

Not to mention convincing.

The way the man was standing, his tone, despite reflecting obvious pain, was confident in his skill set and his threats.

Kenneth wished there had been a deputy cruiser closer to their location but when he'd called into the department, almost everyone had been responding to a nasty wreck out on the county road. Rerouting a couple of cars would take a few minutes. Maybe if he could get the man to talk…

"You have five seconds before you're the only one standing," the man added, certainty in his words. "Five. Four. Three."

"Fine." Kenneth shook his head. "Leave. But I'm not lowering my weapon. Willa, stand up and get behind me."

The man didn't seem to find the directive displeasing. He started slowly moving toward the door, never taking his aim away. There was movement behind Kenneth as he turned, letting him know that Willa was also following directions. By the time the man was about to escape, Kenneth felt the soft touch of her hands on his lower back.

"Leave the gun," Kenneth commanded.

The man shook his head.

Kenneth fired his own weapon.

Willa screamed as the man returned fire.

It turned out he wasn't fast. He also wasn't a great shot. At least, not after being hit in the shoulder by Kenneth's bullet.

His squeezing the trigger was as sloppy as his aim. The man's bullet embedded somewhere in the wall behind them. His gun clattered to the floor and he was out the door, running.

"Stay here," Kenneth yelled at Willa as he followed the man out, gun high. "Barricade the door behind me and don't open it for anyone else."

Willa let out a soft okay.

Kenneth was at the stairs and yelling for the man to stop.

He wasn't listening.

On solid ground, he ran off into the backyard without any indication that he was ready to slow down despite being shot.

Kenneth wasn't going to let him get away.

He jumped the last few steps leading to the concrete of the driveway and was on the man's heels.

They tore through Willa's sister's yard and right into the side yard of the neighbor behind her. A small wood fence was up ahead. If the man wanted to flee, he was going to have to jump it.

That would give Kenneth enough time to close the gap between them.

But the man made a startling choice. Instead of jumping the small fence, he barreled through it.

The crack of the wood against his legs made Kenneth inadvertently flinch.

"Stop! Or I'll shoot," Kenneth yelled out.

The man made no move to listen. His pace even picking up as he ran through the remainder of the yard and into the street.

A stitch pulled at Kenneth's side. Where he'd been hit across his face throbbed in pain. It had been a while since he'd run this hard. It had been a while since his veins had been filled with nothing but adrenaline.

That didn't mean he could keep chasing the man indefinitely. He needed to end the pursuit sooner rather than later.

As Kenneth approached the street, he tried to remember the layout of the neighborhood. Maybe there was a way to cut the man off if he—

The sound of a car's brakes locking up screeched through the air.

A heartbeat later, that same car slammed into the ski-masked man. Like the fence, he became the object that gave.

His body rolled up onto the car's hood and crunched into the windshield. The driver yelled out. When the vehicle stopped, both Kenneth and the driver watched as the man tumbled onto the asphalt.

"Sheriff's department," Kenneth yelled out to the driver. "Stay inside!"

The driver did as he was told as Kenneth converged on the masked man. This time there were no surprises. Willa's attacker was down and out for the count.

THE SIRENS CAME, along with Kelby Creek law, but Willa stayed put in her apartment. The man had broken her door so, as the detective had suggested, she'd barricaded it. First with a kitchen stool, then with an armchair that she'd pulled along the floor.

The same floor she had been pinned against.

She stood back and stared at the door, her phone clutched in one hand, her other hand trailing across her neck where a man's gloved hand had been.

Willa didn't cry.

But she didn't move, either.

Not until she heard it.

Footsteps rushing up the stairs. Heavy and belonging to one person.

"Willa?" That person called through the door. "It's Kenneth. Detective Gray."

That's all she needed to hear.

Willa pulled the armchair back enough to give the detective room to push inside.

She didn't bother moving the stool out of the way and he certainly didn't wait for her to move it.

"Are you okay?" he asked, closing the space between

them, hands going up to her face but not touching it. Instead his hands hovered, concern in his eyes.

"Is he—? Did you get him?"

The detective nodded.

"The first two responding deputies are with him now on the street over." He motioned with his head in the direction he'd chased down the man. "I came back to make sure you were okay. Are you?" His gaze dropped to her neck. There must have been a mark. His brows drew together even more. He was upset. Just as he had been when he'd saved her.

"You came." She didn't answer his question but maybe because she wasn't sure how to. A part of her felt numb. Shock, maybe.

Detective Gray nodded. "You were in trouble," he said. "Of course I came."

Willa knew that, logically, rescuing people who called for it was part of the job when it came to law enforcement. That she was no different, just as her savior had reacted the same way his colleagues might.

Yet the part of Willa that was so close to shaking inside couldn't stop seeing the detective in front of her, ordering her to stay behind him, and only shooting when he knew that he was blocking her body with his.

And then he'd come back for her.

Full of concern, dark eyes running over her, trying to find out if there was something he could fix. Something he could help with.

Willa didn't realize what she was going to do until it was already happening.

She pushed up on her tiptoes and her lips pressed

against the detective's with what she could only describe later as reflex. She wrapped her arms around his neck to anchor her there, anchor her against him, and let the weight of what had happened and her appreciation move through her lips to his.

The detective didn't move right away. They were still in an embrace that neither had expected.

But then he broke the kiss, using his hands to take her upper arms and gently move back.

Willa might have felt the pang of embarrassment or rejection, but the moment the cool air from her apartment, the apartment that had just been violated, hit her lips, the part of her that Willa had been holding off broke through.

Tears didn't start to prick at the corners of her eyes. They came out like waterfalls, rushing down her cheeks as her chest tightened and her breathing became hitched.

Her neck hurt, her leg hurt, her wrist hurt, her apartment was trashed, and she was afraid.

Willa hung her head.

Detected Gray didn't say a word.

But he didn't need to. Not when his hands dropped from her shoulders and, instead of pulling away, he pulled her against him.

She felt his chin rest on top of her hair as Willa lost it completely.

Her body racked against his with sobs, yet the detective didn't move.

He held her against him as though he knew that he was the only thing keeping her up.

That was good. Because he was.

THE NEIGHBORHOOD BECAME a cacophony of sound. It seemed that half of the responding deputies weren't communicating with the other half. Some went to the house and the garage apartment, some went to the street behind where the man had been hit, and others scoured each street. Looking for what, or who, he didn't know.

But he wasn't bothered. Not with what had happened or what he knew would happen next. He simply stood in his backyard, staring at a pool float shaped like a flamingo, and marveling at how some people's timing was impeccable while others' was far from it.

"Honey?"

He turned around at the sound of his wife's voice. The smile he reserved for his home life pulled the corners of his lips up.

"Yes, dear?"

She had a dishtowel in one hand and her phone in the other. She used the former to cover the receiver of the latter. That meant she was about to tell him some gossip that she'd just learned.

"Mrs. Appleton said she just saw the ambulance take a man away. The burglar Tim hit with his car."

"Is he alive?" The chain of information from two streets over wasn't always accurate. What one person would swear to be true, another would swear to be false. It made everything more challenging but wading through the verbal muck to get to the truth was a worthwhile challenge if it meant keeping you alive and free. The ability to get the facts and stay ahead of everyone else seemed to be something the man who'd been dumb enough to get hit by a car in a neighborhood that had a speed limit of twenty miles per hour hadn't possessed.

"As far as Mrs. Appleton is concerned, yes. But she said she heard he wasn't moving much when they put him on the stretcher before they got him into the ambulance."

He shook his head, his wife's eyes still trained on him.

"It's a dang shame something like this could happen in our neighborhood," he decided to say. "It looks like I'll be double-checking the batteries on our alarm system today."

His wife nodded with fervor.

She had no idea the things he could do to her without batting an eye.

Instead, she looked at him like he was the only man in the world who could completely protect her.

That smile that he saved for his personal life grew.

"I'll be in in a second," he added. "I need to make one more call."

She nodded and was back on the phone with Mrs. Appleton in a flash.

Until he was sure she was on the other side of the house, he listened to the sirens moving off into the distance.

Then he took the piece of fabric out of his pocket.

Despite the years that had gone by, the bloodstain was as dark as it had been the day it had first been soaked.

He sighed into the afternoon air. It smelled like rain.

Rain was good.
It had a way of making everyone forget.
And what the rain wouldn't do, he would.

Chapter Seven

The sky was dark.

It matched everyone's moods.

Willa absently rubbed at her neck. She picked through the wreckage in her apartment, trying to assess the damage. She'd heard a deputy who'd seemed friendly with Detective Gray, say what had happened looked like a smash-and-grab. One that she had interrupted, despite trying her best to hide.

The detective didn't seem as convinced. Then again, Willa didn't know him well enough to understand all of his expressions. Had she been a betting woman, though, she didn't think he believed the man in the ski mask had had such a simple task in mind.

Or maybe Willa was projecting.

The most expensive items she owned were more or less intact. The man hadn't brought a bag or anything else to carry his stolen loot with. Instead, he'd turned her home over without so much as lifting her computer, her TV, or even her jewelry, which had been out in the open on the top of her chest of drawers.

Not to mention he had broken in during the daylight

hours, while her car was parked in the driveway, and he'd brought a gun.

If that was a simple smash-and-grab, she'd hate to see what a more complex operation looked like.

Willa walked back to her bedroom again. She knew that Martha would be there soon and if she saw the mess and the mark around Willa's neck, she would lose it. So while the detective finished up with another Dawn County Sheriff's Department colleague, she started to straighten the room as best she could.

She didn't make it far. After coming across a jewelry dish that her mother had made her a few birthdays ago, broken in pieces on the floor, Willa sat on her bed and tried not to cry again.

If she had any more tears left, that is.

After kissing the detective, it seemed every tear she had in her had poured out onto the man.

If she cried now, it would just be her going through the movements without the mess.

A little knock pulled her attention from the broken dish to the bedroom's doorway. She felt a flush come over her as she locked eyes with the man who had saved her.

"Detective," she greeted.

He put his hand up to stop her.

"Please, call me Kenneth, Miss Tate."

Willa smiled at that. "Please, call me Willa, Kenneth."

He returned the small dose of humor with a nod. "Will do." His eyes went from her to the room around them, scanning the mess. He did that a lot. Looked around, like he was building a catalog in his mind. He was probably good at the details, which only made him that much better at his job.

He also had proved to be quick on his feet.

"You got here really fast," Willa noted. "After we talked on the phone, I was sure it would take you longer to get here. I also thought you'd wait for backup."

Kenneth was modest about it. He shrugged. "I was actually already looking for you when you answered my last call. It was lucky that I wasn't that far away."

Heat, pleasant and at the same time uncomfortable, rose into her cheeks. She smiled.

"It's a good thing you wanted to meet today." Willa felt her smile flip. She gave the man a questioning look. "I haven't had the chance to ask, but why did you want to meet?"

Kenneth didn't seem excited about his answer. Still, he gave it.

"I wanted to ask you some more questions about Josiah Linderman. And I wanted to take another look at the box—"

Willa jumped up and winced at the pain in her leg.

Her focus, however, pinpointed on the one thing she should have already thought about.

In that moment, she felt like a fool.

"The box! Of course, I'd forgotten about the dang box!"

She rushed back into the living room, purpose driving her heels into the floor. Everyone from the sheriff's department was gone, but still she lowered her voice when she got to the window seat.

"I haven't told my sister, or anyone, about me look-ing into Josiah Linderman or this box," she explained. "Martha is really nosy sometimes, not that that's al-ways a bad thing, but sometimes that nosiness gets her to snooping into my stuff."

Willa lowered herself to her knees and bent over the side of the open window seat. Her hair swung down in her face but she didn't need to see to know exactly where the box was. She reached out to the farthest left corner that she could access and felt the worn wood beneath her hand.

When she pulled it out, she couldn't help but feel a little guilty about having a hiding place specifically from her sister.

"Since I found this, I've been putting it in here and covering it with blankets." She motioned to the quilt she'd hurriedly thrown out as she'd gotten inside the window seat to hide from the intruder. "Martha may like to snoop, but if it's too much trouble, she doesn't bother herself with it. So, at least as far as I know, she never found the box and no one else knows it exists."

Kenneth gave her a look she couldn't quite deci-pher. She led him to the counter, where she put the box on its top.

"If you're wondering about my thought process on why I hid this and didn't tell anyone about it, let me re-mind you that Kelby Creek doesn't have the greatest track record when it comes to mysteries. I mean dur-ing the last two years there have been some really wild ones that have overtaken the town." Willa tapped the top of the box. "I was hoping I could solve one by myself without getting caught in something slightly terrifying. In my mind that could happen if I was the only one who knew about it."

"To be honest, that is a very fair point when it comes to Kelby Creek," Kenneth conceded.

He didn't open the box right away.

Willa watched as his expression changed again to an emotion she couldn't read. She was about to ask him point-blank what he was thinking, but he pulled the lid open before she could.

Willa's gaze stayed on his expression before falling to his lips and staying there for half a second too long. She hadn't addressed the fact that she had kissed him and he hadn't addressed the fact that he'd held her for a long while before his colleagues had showed up. Maybe because they both knew it was an overflow of emotions brought on by a traumatic event, but Willa found that a great big part of her wanted to feel the man against her again. To feel his warmth and steadiness. To feel his heart beating at a steady rhythm against hers, reminding her at every beat that he was there.

But while she was daydreaming about his touch and how it had made her feel safe, Kenneth became rigid with tension.

Willa looked down at the box.

She gasped.

"Judging by your reaction, I'm assuming you're not the one who took the piece of fabric out, are you?" Kenneth's voice wasn't cold but it was clipped. Professional. He was back to being Detective Gray.

"No. I didn't," she answered. Willa's palms became

sweaty. She felt sick. "No one knows about the box, just like I already said. And I was already hiding with it when that man first broke in. He had no time to take that cloth. How was it gone if he didn't take it and no one else knew about it?"

Kenneth shook his head.

"If this box contained evidence of an unsolved murder, then outside of you and me there is at least one other person who knows what was and is supposed to be in here." He gave her a long look. How she wished she could be in his arms instead of on the receiving end of words that chilled her to the bone. "The killer."

"His name is Leonard Bartow and he's been a nuisance to this department since before The Flood."

Deputy Carlos Park had made a face when he'd said the man's name and that off-key expression only soured further as he'd said "The Flood."

Kenneth had no doubt he didn't look happy, either, at the mention of the latter, to be fair.

The Flood was a town-wide nickname for the disaster that had created a rift between the locals and those in positions of authority years before. Friends, families and neighbors had all gone from trusting those with a badge or influence to automatically assuming they were part of the conspiracy surrounding the abduction of Annie McHale, the daughter of one of the most beloved families in Kelby Creek. Or that those same people were crooked in some other way.

It was the main reason why so many closed cases needed reevaluating and why any cold case related to those who had been caught in the conspiracy were being reopened and double-checked.

Never mind the remaining cold cases that had never been solved even once.

It was why the unit Kenneth headed, and solely ran for the time being, had been created.

The Dawn County Sheriff's Department was still understaffed almost three years after The Flood.

It needed someone with singular focus and drive. Someone to help without distraction. Someone who had a unique motivation to find justice for those no longer around to seek it themselves.

"Does he make a habit of attacking women in their homes during broad daylight?" Kenneth's voice came out in a low growl.

Deputy Park sighed and crossed his arms over his chest.

"If he does, it didn't show up in any reports or complaints," he answered. "His track record in Kelby Creek over the last decade has been burglary. Unarmed at that. He went into offices, cars and residential homes when no one was around, grabbed the most valuable things he could, and then was gone. The only way we even knew it was him half of the time was through security or home cameras and eyewitnesses after he left. He might seem sloppy while he's doing his thing, but after he leaves a place, it's like he simply disappears into thin air. *Poof.*"

"But he has a record."

Deputy Park nodded. "Before he went *poof*, he was

caught twice within three years. Spent some time in prison for it."

"And now he's strangling women and carrying a gun," Kenneth said with a snarl.

"It seems like it."

They took a moment of silence to think on that. A few deputies who had responded to his call for backup were behind them, chatting and enjoying their break. A few doors down, Willa and the sheriff were finishing up her official statement in the department's meeting room.

He wished he had a way to erase the last few hours from her memory, but knew trauma wasn't something one could just wish away. Instead, he focused on what he could.

"The car they found a few blocks away, which they think is his, you said it had several items in it that were stolen?"

Deputy Park nodded again. "It's looking like he broke into two other houses up and down the same street before he got to Miss Tate. Some of the items were in the car when we found it."

"Do you have a catalog of the items? Or a picture?" Kenneth wondered if the fabric from the box had been inside, even though Willa had been adamant that there was no way Leonard would have had the time to get it while she was there.

Regardless, it wouldn't hurt to look.

"Yeah, we have some pictures that Gordon took. Want to see them?"

Kenneth said he would.

It didn't take long after that to start wrapping the day

up. He went to his office and finished what he could before grabbing his things and heading to the meeting room. It was good timing; the sheriff was coming out.

He wasn't in a good mood at all. No one was a fan of what had happened that afternoon. He was quick to give his recap of his thoughts but then patted Kenneth on the shoulder and said he had to deal with the press.

"The whole town will know by tomorrow about what happened. I better get prepared."

Kenneth didn't envy that side of the job and told the sheriff good luck.

He popped his head inside the meeting room as soon as the man was gone and locked eyes with the woman he'd been worrying about since that morning.

Willa was standing, cell phone in her hand.

She looked lost.

"Everything all right?" Kenneth knew it wasn't, but he had to say the words.

A strained smile righted itself across her lips.

"Just tired, I think. Maybe a little overwhelmed, too."

Kenneth didn't like the way she sounded. He didn't like the mark around her neck. He didn't like the way she was putting up a front of smiles and being accommodating when she was the one who had been attacked.

It made him feel…protective.

And he hadn't felt that in a long time.

"Do you need a ride home?"

Willa nodded but held up her phone. "Kimball told me to call when I was finished here."

Kimball Smith, Kenneth knew, was Willa's brother-in-law. He'd been the first to arrive on scene outside of law enforcement back at the apartment. Without announcing who he was, he had picked Willa up in a hug and spun her in a half circle. It was only after Willa returned the embrace with several assurances that she was okay that she introduced the two of them. Before she'd done so, Kenneth couldn't get around the fact that he hadn't known if Willa Tate was seeing anyone. Sure, her online profiles might have said "single," but that didn't mean she hadn't been dating anyone.

Now he didn't have to guess on it. She all but told him the only people who would be calling after her were her sister, her brother-in-law, her friend Ebony, and the people she worked with. Anyone else would be after gossip.

"My shift just ended," Kenneth surprised himself by saying. "If you don't mind, I'd like to give you a ride."

It might have been his imagination, but Willa's shoulders dropped a little, like the tension in them had lessened.

"That would really be nice," she said. "I think Kimball and Martha are actually out buying a new security system right now. So, yeah, if you don't mind, that would be great."

"I promise I don't. Come on. Let's get out of here."

Chapter Eight

It had already started raining in some parts of Kelby Creek.

Willa could smell it in the air.

Normally, that would have been a topic of conversation. An easy one to make with someone you barely knew, especially while in the car with them. Yet she kept quiet about it. The urge to dish out her Southern niceties was gone.

A rare occurrence for her.

Instead, she'd remained silent after the detective had finished his quick call before leaving the parking lot.

Kenneth, however, didn't seem to like the silence. He spoke the moment he started driving. "So, did the sheriff tell you about Leonard Bartow?"

Willa fought the urge to touch her neck. An EMT had told her in her driveway that she was lucky her attacker hadn't been stronger and that Kenneth had showed up when he had. A bruise was much preferable than more extensive damage that could be caused in that area. At least she could talk without it hurting. Apparently, that wasn't always the case.

The thought made Willa wholly uncomfortable just thinking about the what-ifs.

"Yes," she answered. "He said that Leonard has a history of breaking into people's houses and stealing. He also said that today's stop at my apartment was his third break-in. Leonard must have expected me to be in the main house and not the garage apartment, which is why he attacked."

Out of her periphery, Willa saw Kenneth turn toward her.

"But you don't believe that." It was a statement. One that was true.

"I stand by what I said. There is no way Leonard got that fabric when he broke into my place. He couldn't have. I was literally pressed up against the box. *But* I don't think him being there was a coincidence. He was in my apartment for almost half an hour. Why? It's not that big a space and all of my valuables? They were just out in the open, ready to be taken. So what was he doing?"

"Do think he was waiting for you?" Kenneth's voice had gone flat.

Willa was glad to shake her head.

"If he was waiting for me, he picked a weird time to do it. My normal workday is until five and going to my house before I was supposed to meet you was a last-minute decision." Willa looked down at her sundress. It seemed so silly now that she'd gone through so much all because of wanting to wear a dress to impress the man next to her.

She shook her head again. "He had to be there about the box, right? It's too much of a coincidence not to be."

Kenneth was thoughtful when he responded.

"The timing of it all does make it more suspect. He put himself at a lot of risk to seemingly do nothing. Just breaking into a place that has a car parked outside is dangerous. Even if he might have thought the car belonged to someone in the main house. Not only did he do that, he did it during the day and then he stayed. I can't tell if he had a plan or if he's not the brightest tool in the toolshed. Either way, it's all definitely suspicious."

"It also makes it slightly terrifying." They slowed to stop at a light. She shared a glance with him before looking down at her hands. "Let's say Leonard didn't know about the box at all… Then who took the cloth?"

Kenneth didn't have an answer. Not that Willa had expected one. In fact, she hadn't expected anything from the man after their meeting on Monday.

"You called today because you wanted to talk. Does that mean you found something about Josiah?"

Kenneth's eyes were back on the road. They didn't stray her way as she studied his profile. His jaw was hard, his brow pronounced with concentration, and his lips were warm. At least they had been when she'd kissed him.

But that was part of a different conversation Willa wanted to have with the man. Not the one she needed at the moment.

"I didn't find anything on Josiah but, after talking to the sheriff and thinking on it some more, I wanted to see if you could walk me through what you've done since finding the box."

"You mean my investigation?"

Willa saw the corner of his lips twitch like he was holding in a smile.

"Yeah. I want to make sure I'm on the same page with you before I go any further."

Hope sprang eternal in Willa's chest. "So, you're officially taking on Josiah's case?"

"More like I'm going to try to figure out what's going on with that box."

Willa was pleased as punch about that. She smiled wide.

"Either way, I'm glad to hear it. I was starting to feel like one of those killers on a TV show. You know, the ones who have like a weird shrine of pictures or a bulletin board with tons of strings attached to it."

"Believe me, you're no killer."

Embarrassment took heat from Willa's stomach and pushed it up into her cheeks.

She hadn't met Kenneth before yet, as a local, she knew about the murder of his wife. There might have been the odd homicide in Kelby Creek and Dawn County but the killing of a young woman out jogging with no leads? That had been on repeat on the news.

And, if she had somehow managed to miss that, then Kenneth taking the job as the head of the cold case unit had put the story back into circulation.

Willa's heart squeezed at her poor choice of words.

"I… I'm sorry," she tried to rectify by saying. "I didn't mean to—"

Kenneth held up his hand to stop her. "It's okay. No harm done."

Willa wasn't sure it hadn't been, but she didn't say so. She quieted while the rain picked up and blurred the world around them. It helped her thoughts from sticking where they shouldn't.

That didn't last long.

Willa glanced over at the man's hand. She'd already noted his lack of wedding band on his ring finger when she'd first met him. Still, she felt the need to check again. Instead, her eyes stopped at the holster on his hip.

She must have made a noise.

Kenneth turned to her in a flash. "What?"

Willa had already blushed twice since being in the SUV with Kenneth. And for different reasons. Now she did it a third time.

Not for embarrassment or the prickling desire she suspected she was starting to have for the detective. But for the shame of overlooking the most important detail from the mystery she was trying to solve.

She gave Kenneth a long look.

"You're probably not going to like this."

THANKFULLY, THE CAR ride had been over quickly after Willa's ominous statement.

That didn't mean that Kenneth had parked the SUV in her driveway and then led the way to the garage apartment without apprehension. It was there when they walked inside of the living space that he noted that the apartment had been straightened and cleaned since earlier. When Willa turned around to face him her gaze never wavered from his as she bottom-lined why they were there.

"There used to be a gun in the box."

Kenneth ran his hand over the stubble along his jaw. He repeated her words to make sure he'd heard them right. Willa nodded.

He would have sighed in exasperation, maybe even anger, had it been anyone else who had just dropped a bombshell like that.

Instead he kept his cool. Though he had some questions.

"Why didn't you tell me when you first came to the department? That's a pretty big detail to leave out. A gun would've certainly gotten my attention a lot faster."

Willa rung her hands together. Her cheeks had turned a rosy shade again. Just as they had in his SUV. It only made part of him feel even more protective of her. Being in the room where she'd been attacked was only making that feeling stronger.

"Well, I was trying to figure out this whole situation before coming to the department in first place, since I didn't know who to trust. I mean, I know that the sheriff's department isn't like the one before The Flood, but there's just so much water that hasn't actually gone under that bridge for us locals. And... I don't know, I just didn't want to chance missing out on getting some kind of justice or answers for Josiah's family."

"So you didn't tell me about the gun because you didn't know if you could trust us. Trust me."

Willa shrugged. Those rosy cheeks became rosier.

"Well, yeah," she said. "That and the fact I didn't

exactly want to bring a gun, even if it wasn't loaded, into a sheriff's department. So I decided to kind of feel you out first."

He put his hands on his hips and slid his eyebrow up question.

"You decided to feel me out first," he repeated, slightly humored.

A quick smile passed over her lips before deepening into a frown.

"Yes. But then you kind of dismissed me, so I decided not to bring up the gun. When you called me today to meet, I was going to tell you then. Or, at least, I think I would've. The day kind of got away from me, and not in the best way, as you know."

Kenneth noted the way her hand flexed. He bet she was keeping it at waist level with thoughtful intention. He'd already caught her several times lightly brushing the bruised skin of her neck.

The sight of her trying to control the reflex made his disbelief that she hadn't told him about the weapon soften. He let out a breath, purposely loosening his shoulders.

"So you found the gun and then you hid the gun," he stated. "Where is it now?"

Before they had gone into the department for Willa to give her official statement, she and Kenneth had decided to find a different place to put the box. At first, he'd suggested taking it to the department. But with Willa's adamant insistence about keeping it, despite the break-in, he'd relented. There was just something about the tear tracks down her cheeks and her bloodshot eyes that made him want to give her everything she wanted. Or, at a minimum, not add to her current stress.

They'd moved the box from the window seat to, of all places, the refrigerator. He had laughed at the suggestion but realized in hindsight that it had been a pretty good place to hide something. How many people with bad intentions broke into a home and went through the fridge?

He chuckled to himself as she went to the freezer portion of the refrigerator and opened the door. She looked inside and breathed a sigh of relief so loudly that Kenneth found another bit of tension fall away from his shoulders.

"It's in there?" He walked over and stopped at her shoulder.

Willa actually clapped. "Yes. Thank goodness!"

She moved aside as Kenneth pulled on the latex gloves he'd taken from the trunk of his vehicle. No matter what he drove, he always carried them around everywhere.

"Is…is that it?"

At the back of the freezer, next to a box of Toaster Strudel, sat a large Tupperware container. Through its clear sides, he saw something black inside.

Willa crossed her arms over her chest, defensive.

"Hey, watch that tone. I wasn't going to put a gun willy-nilly in my freezer. What do you take me for? An amateur?"

Kenneth was going to comment that that's exactly what she was, but glanced over in time to see her smirk. She was teasing him.

When she saw that he understood she was playing with him, she shrugged again.

"Plus, I'm a good Southern woman. One thing we have in spades are plastic containers. I've used them for leftovers, sewing needles and thread, chocolate-covered whatevers, and one time to catch a lizard and use it to put him outside. Why not add hiding a gun in the freezer to the list?"

Kenneth reached inside and gently pulled the Tupperware out.

"You know, I've heard and seen a lot of things during my time in law enforcement," he said. "But I can tell you with certainty that's the first time I've heard, and the first time I've seen, this."

Kenneth decided not to inspect the gun then and there. By her own admission, Willa had already done her own investigation, at least, as much as she could. He also decided, even if she wouldn't admit it, that Willa was exhausted. He didn't want to keep her from eating with her family and getting some rest.

He walked her downstairs to the side door that led into her sister's house, promising that he would look into the gun.

"My house is currently being worked on, so I have to take off tomorrow to meet with the contractor. But I can still look into this—" he tapped the lid of the container "—from home. I'd also like to talk to you about what you already know in more detail. If you don't mind waiting until Friday or, if you do, I can get you in with Detective Lovett or—"

"Or I can come over tomorrow morning with coffee and tell you all about it then?"

Kenneth was caught off guard by the offer, but not as much as how he felt about it.

On the one hand, he knew Willa's intentions were pure. She wanted to find out what had happened to Josiah Linderman while understanding every single thing about the box's contents. If he turned down her suggestion, he had every confidence in the world she would show up Friday morning bright and early.

But she didn't want to wait.

He could see that in her face, her movements, how she looked at the gun hidden in the container in his hand.

And Kenneth knew that feeling. The impatience that ate at you when all you wanted to do was to move forward but instead got stuck waiting.

He didn't want that for her. Just like he didn't want to be the one to put her through that simply because of something he had scheduled before meeting her. A meeting about pipes to boot.

On the other hand, he couldn't help but wonder if Willa had picked up on his shifting feelings for her.

From a stranger with an interesting story to a woman he barely knew and still felt the almost primal urge to protect.

And that was before they had kissed.

Willa put up her hands to stop him before he responded. "I don't want to overstep and I don't want to encroach on your day off," she hurriedly added. "I just want to show you that I appreciate what you're doing with a cup of coffee and a stress-free atmosphere."

She laughed. "Though, I guess cold cases, guns in freezers, and a relative stranger trying to come to your house doesn't exactly equal a stress-free atmosphere."

Kenneth knew the moment that she laughed what his answer was going to be.

"If you don't mind a construction zone, a very hyper golden retriever, and me asking you more questions than a dad asks his daughter's date before her prom, then that's fine by me."

Willa's lips stretched wide.

The rain was still falling around them just beyond the awning. Still, even without the contrast, Kenneth was sure she'd be just as bright.

"Sounds like a plan," she said. "Just text me your address and your coffee preference, and I'll be there come rain or shine."

Kenneth agreed to the plan. He was ready to head out into the rain and back to his SUV when Willa reached out and caught his elbow.

"Kenneth?"

He stopped and readjusted his gaze down to hers.

She was back to being solemn, lips downturned, and thoughts he couldn't hear weighing against her.

"Yeah?"

She didn't let go of his arm.

"Do you think Leonard Bartow broke into my apartment earlier to take the fabric only to come back later looking for the gun? Do you think it was all a coincidence? Bad luck on my part?"

Kenneth didn't say anything but he'd already gone through the same questions in his head. The last he'd heard, Leonard was in stable condition and Detective Lovett had already made plans to talk to him the moment he was conscious and able. Kenneth had also gone through the pictures found in Leonard's car. Nothing had been remotely linked to Willa, the box, or Josiah.

But someone had taken the piece of fabric.

And whether Kenneth believed in coincidence or not, he absolutely knew that bad luck could and did happen to good people.

"I don't know. But I can promise you this, I'm certainly going to find out. Starting with calling up Mae's brother and seeing if we can't find out more about the day Josiah Linderman went missing."

Chapter Nine

Willa knew that she had what some would call a bubbly personality. Again, that was another thing she could blame on her almost compulsive need to be polite. You catch more flies with honey than vinegar, and all of that. It wasn't until she was older that she'd realized she wasn't sure if that's who she was. The peppy blonde who laughed at jokes, worried if you'd eaten enough, and never had to borrow sugar from a neighbor because her cabinet was stocked with it.

Was that really her? Or had she fallen into a stereotype that she'd accidentally built because she thought it was what was expected of her?

Willa couldn't say for sure and it wasn't until she'd found the box and had done some digging that she'd even begun to wonder if she could be, or wanted to be, something else. Some*one* else.

She was parked at the curb outside Kenneth's house, once again asking herself the same questions that had been revolving through her mind the last month.

Introspection while holding a coffee caddy in a Mazda with a notable dent on the passenger-side door where a Walmart customer had unapologetically run into it with their cart. Even then, Willa had smiled, promised it was okay, and then gone on to put away stray carts from the spot next to hers.

She looked out the front window and wondered what Kenneth would have done in the same situation.

The smell of coffee warmed her.

This had been Willa's idea and now she was stalling.

She should've waited until Friday and not put the man on the spot and forced him to help her. At least, not help her from his home.

Willa tried to give herself a mental pep talk to get moving but before the gears could start turning, someone rapped against her window.

She jumped and turned to the confused face of someone familiar.

"Landon?"

Willa opened the door and Landon Mitchell stood back as she got out. A flush crossed her cheeks, if only for the fact she hadn't even thought of the possibility of running into her ex-boyfriend here of all places.

"Landon," she repeated. "What are you doing here?"

Her friend Ebony had once told her that she hadn't found love yet because of the first man Ebony had ever gotten into serious relationship with. Ebony had lamented repeatedly about how, no matter who she'd dated after, she couldn't help but compare him to her first love. From personality right on down to shoes.

"Sometimes you just meet a man who sticks," Ebony had said with a shake of her head. "And once that guy sticks, you can't help but put him up against every man you meet."

For all intents and purposes, Landon should have been that man for Willa. He'd been the longest relationship she'd ever had and the only one where marriage had been considered. Not to mention they'd lived together the last year of their relationship. He should have been whom she pictured, whether she meant to or not.

But wouldn't you know it, instead of listening for his answer, she was retroactively comparing him against someone else.

Landon was almost the same height as Kenneth but built in a completely different way. He was thick with muscle from hours at the gym and a job that often required manual labor. Kenneth, on the other hand, was lean and toned. A lithe man who was strong *and* fast. Someone who sat behind a desk but who also could chase down a suspect in a flash. Then there was Landon's highlighted features that people first noticed when meeting him. Light green eyes, like grass after a rain, copper-blond hair that shagged this way and that, and a set of cheek dimples that flexed even if he was barely smiling. These were all details Willa had appreciated during their relationship.

Yet, there she was. Standing, with a coffee caddy in hand, in front of a man everyone thought she'd marry— herself included, if she was being honest—and thinking about… Eyes the color of deep blue water, hair cut close but just long enough to run her fingers through, and a seriousness to the way he smiled that gave off an edge with a vulnerability to it.

She might have loved Landon but, in a surprise that was making her cheeks burn, Willa realized she wasn't just at the detective's house because she wanted answers for a cold case.

She wanted Kenneth Gray.

And what a thing to come to realize while staring at her ex.

Landon's green-grass stare coupled with an eyebrow quirk. He pointed over her shoulder to Kenneth's house. "I have a meeting with Mr. Gray about his house."

"Oh my gosh! I didn't even put that together when Kenneth said he had a contractor coming over."

Of course, he would have hired a local contractor. It didn't hurt that Landon was good at his job, either.

"Kenneth, huh? Why are *you* here, Willa?"

Willa's defenses flared at his tone. She was not a fan of that one.

She squared her shoulders and held the caddy a little higher.

"I'm here to talk with my friend and drink some coffee," she said, sidestepping the truth. If she still hadn't told her sister about the box and Josiah Linderman, there was no way she was about to tell Landon.

"Aren't you supposed to be at work?" he challenged. "I know for a fact that Clanton is working two sites in town. Y'all have to be busy."

"I took the day off, thank you very much."

That eyebrow of his went higher, if possible.

If he'd heard what had happened at her apartment the night before with Leonard Bartow, she was sure he would've already commented on it. Instead, he was looking like he was getting wound up about who she was fraternizing with. Something she surely did not appreciate from anyone, let alone an engaged man.

Landon must have sensed he was straying near dangerous territory. He raised his hands in defense.

"Now don't go getting all squirrely on me, Willa. I was just curious is all. I haven't really seen you around town and here you are just sitting in the car outside of my client's house. You can't blame a guy for asking what's going on."

There was that polite prodding again. Willa decided to let his not-so-subtle poking pass.

"Well, how about instead of us standing here gabbing, we go in there so you can get to that client of yours?"

Landon conceded, but there was a hesitation to it. Like he wanted to say more but ultimately chose not to. Instead, he helped her get her bag out of the car and then walked with her up to the front porch.

She decided not to say anything as he stepped in front of her to knock on the door.

They lapsed into a somewhat awkward silence until Kenneth appeared.

It was the first time Willa had seen the man dressed down. It certainly wasn't a disappointing sight.

Landon cleared his throat before extending his hand.

"Good morning, Mr. Gray. Sorry again for the delay getting over here. I had an issue at this house in the county over because of all the rain from yesterday. Then I had to catch up a little with Willa here."

"That's no problem," Kenneth replied, shaking his

hand. He shared a look with Willa but stepped aside to motion them both in without addressing her directly. "How about I show you around the house and we talk about what I think I want done?"

"That works for me." Landon's gaze switched to Willa, as did Kenneth's.

"Willa, if you don't mind, you can make yourself at home in my office." Kenneth nodded toward the door at the end of the first-floor hallway they were standing in. "Delilah will probably love the company. I shouldn't be long."

Willa's customer service smile must have been a flashing neon light. Both men seemed to hover over it as she nodded. "Sure thing!"

She handed his coffee over and then was off to the office without any more conversation between them. And that was good because she didn't really know what else to say.

While the last month had had many twists and turns she hadn't seen coming, standing in Kenneth's home between him and Landon Mitchell had never even entered her mind as a possible scenario. She was glad to escape and hang out in the detective's office.

Even more so when a ball of golden fur and excitement met her at the door.

"You must be Delilah." Willa laughed as the dog's tail whipped back and forth faster at the mention of her name. "Well, Delilah, my name is Willa, and I am very pleased to talk with you and not with the two of them."

Delilah seemed to agree, especially when her tummy became the target of a good belly rub.

MR. MITCHELL GLANCED at the office door one too many times before he left. Kenneth thanked him for coming, after they'd gone through a standard recap of what happened next, before each half waved goodbye and went his separate way.

Before the contractor made it to his truck, he gave Willa's car one long look.

Kenneth paused by the front window to see the man drive off and then went to his office.

When he opened the door, he found himself pausing again.

His office wasn't at all like the one he used at the sheriff's department. This one was filled with books, art and knickknacks, pictures of family and friends, and a desk his father had built. The couch opposite the desk was the one his wife had insisted on buying so she could lounge and chat while he worked.

Since her passing, he'd gone through the difficult task of donating, storing and rearranging most of the things Ally had left behind. He'd needed it out of the house. He'd needed to not see constant reminders that she wasn't there anymore. His mother had told him, time and time again, it was all in the spirit of moving on and that there was no shame in how he or anyone else grieved. But Kenneth had known what it really was.

He'd needed to give himself space so he didn't drive himself over the edge.

Again.

Because, unlike most widows and widowers, Ally's death hadn't been natural. Or accidental.

She'd been murdered.

And walking into the empty house and seeing her clothes hanging in the closet, her favorite blanket thrown on the couch, and their wedding picture front and center over the fireplace had been a reminder.

Not only was she gone, but the man who'd taken her was still out there somewhere.

Every single day, every single night, every single moment he was in the house, Kenneth had felt that pain and frustration and near-suffocating rage.

That side of him hadn't gone unnoticed either. He'd been told to sell the house by old friends and family, to even leave town to start over somewhere new so the reminders weren't every place he went.

Yet, he could never do it.

Leaving the house, leaving town, didn't erase the fact that Ally was gone. It would just mean that he'd be gone too. Something about that had never sat well with him. He didn't want to leave. He wanted to catch his breath and keep going.

He wanted to heal.

He wanted to find her killer.

Things Kenneth knew he could never do if he left it all behind.

So, he hadn't, and now years later and the house was that of a single man. One with minimal tastes and a need for function over sentimentality.

Yet, the love he had for Ally had been as stubborn as the woman herself. One day he'd walked into his office and there she was. In the artwork on the walls, the books she'd loved nestled on the shelves, and the couch she'd nagged him about getting until he'd finally relented.

And now there was Willa, lying across the same couch and laughing when she saw him.

"In my defense, I didn't know if Delilah was allowed on the furniture so I made an executive decision that she was until you told me otherwise."

Delilah's tail was wagging a mile a minute as she popped up from her spot on Willa's chest and stomach. Kenneth smirked as her big brown eyes tracked him on the way to his desk chair.

"I tried the whole *discipline* thing when I first adopted her," he admitted. "While she may be well-trained out in the real world, when it comes to the inside of this house, she knows she's queen."

Willa seemed entirely amused by that. She sat up on her cushion and readjusted to Delilah's new position for being petted.

"Let me guess, you're the kind of guy who lets his dog sleep with him in his bed, but *also* the kind of guy who would never cop to that fact."

Kenneth shrugged, though she'd pegged him true.

"If I were that kind of guy then, like you said, I'd never admit it."

Willa laughed out loud again, which only made Delilah more excited. She wiggled this way and that before deciding Willa's lap was the best position to lay her head to get her favorite behind-the-ear scratches. Kenneth should have known the two would be a good match. Both were bright spots in a world that could be gray.

"All right, sorry about the delay," he said, getting to the matter at hand. He pulled out his personal notebook, wanting to take more detailed notes than his notepad had room for.

"It's no problem. After yesterday, I decided to take today off." Willa rolled her shoulders in a wave motion. Kenneth quickly glanced at her neck. She didn't miss the attention. "I hid the bruise as best I could with some foundation Martha had for tattoo cover-up. But then I realized how small Kelby Creek is and, bruise or not, the news about the break-in and attack had already spread like wildfire before I'd even gone to sleep last night. So, I decided to give myself a day to breathe, so to speak."

Kenneth felt himself stiffen in anger at Leonard Bartow. The last he'd heard, the man was still unable to speak to anyone. Apparently, he'd hit his head a little too hard to bounce back with ease. Not that Kenneth was upset that he wasn't up and around yet. Though talking to him would get them some answers he wouldn't mind having.

"Does it hurt?" he asked when he realized he was staring.

Willa shook her head. "A little sore but not bad."

Kenneth had every intention to use that to segue to the beginning of her Josiah investigation but couldn't help himself. He averted his gaze to his notebook for a moment and tried to sound nonchalant.

"Did Mr. Mitchell know what happened?" he asked.

"I don't think so. Why? Did he say something?"

Her voice had changed. Not a lot, but the pitch had grown higher than normal. And her words came out faster.

Kenneth met her genuinely curious gaze as he picked up his pen.

"No, that's why I was wondering if he knew," he answered. "With the way you two were outside, and then the way he was looking at you in here, I thought there might be something—" Kenneth waved his pen in the air a little then put it back on the desktop "—there."

Willa outright snorted. Then her cheeks went a shade of crimson he hadn't yet seen on her.

"Sorry if I overstepped," he interjected before she could speak. "It's none of my business."

She waved off his dismissal. Delilah nudged at her hand with her nose.

"No, it's fine. I'm just not used to being around people who don't know about us."

Kenneth didn't like the *us* but knew there was no reason to feel that way. Still, he was glad for the explanation that followed.

"We dated for a few years and lived together for the last one, but it didn't work out. He's a good guy, and a great contractor by the way, but something was just *off* between us. At least for me. So I asked for a break to see if I couldn't sort out what was bothering me and realized I wasn't happier without him but I *also* wasn't sadder." She shrugged. "I thought that was worth a conversation but I guess I waited too long to have it. He started dating someone and then got engaged all before our lease was even up."

Kenneth whistled. "He doesn't waste any time, does he?"

Willa shook her head but she was smiling.

"Not with her, apparently. Though, don't get me wrong, I very much think we're better off as friends."

Even though she was being flippant, Kenneth saw the wounded look cross over her face. He liked it less than the mention of her and Landon as an *us*.

"You deserve someone who you'll miss when they leave a room and someone who will miss you if you leave a room," he said. "Anything less and you're settling for someone else's fantasy."

Willa's eyes widened slightly. Her hand stopped its movement through Delilah's fur. Kenneth worried he had overstepped again but, slowly, the corner of her lips pulled up.

"Why, Detective Gray, that was almost poetry right there."

Kenneth chuckled. "I feel like I should be offended at how surprised you sound, but I'll take the compliment in that instead."

Willa's grin filled out into another one of those bright smiles he'd bet was second nature to her. Just looking at it, at her, and he'd almost suspect she had some kind of superpower. Willa Tate made him feel better with such little effort that his feelings of intrigue for the woman had only multiplied tenfold since their first meeting.

That made her tears as she'd sobbed against his chest yesterday something he never wanted to revisit. Her pain had become his pain.

And that meant he needed to get to the bottom of what had happened to the missing piece of fabric, the contents of the once-buried box, the mystery of the gun, and the disappearance of Josiah Linderman.

Now.

Because, if anything happened to Willa, Kenneth wouldn't forgive himself.

He couldn't.

He picked up his pen and set his jaw.

Willa picked up on the change, he noted, as her fingers stilled atop Delilah's head instead of stroking her fur.

"Now, Willa," he started, voice unintentionally low, "tell me everything. And I mean *everything*."

Chapter Ten

"I have to say, I'm impressed."

Kenneth put down his pen. The first time he'd done so in the last half hour. When he said that he wanted to be thorough in what Willa had learned, he hadn't exaggerated. He taken more notes than she probably had taken all of her college career.

"I actually have half a mind to ask you to join law enforcement," he added on. "I could use a detective like you."

Willa felt her cheeks turn hot at the compliment. Though it wasn't all deserved.

"I worked on trying to figure this out for a month and all I got was the name of a woman in a picture and an idea that a man most think left town was, in fact, killed," she countered. "I'm not sure that constitutes being a good detective."

"Don't sell yourself short. I'm not sure most people would even care to figure out what was going on."

"Probably because most people would take the box straight to the cops when they found a gun inside."

Willa watched as Kenneth conceded, his expression momentarily thoughtful.

"I can see why you didn't, though," he said. "I had worked at the department before The Flood happened and after we saw how far the corruption spread… Well, even I had some reservations about returning."

"Why did you?" Willa found herself starting to want a lot of things when it came to the detective. During her recount of all the people she'd talked to about Mae Linderman's picture and Josiah's disappearance, she'd caught herself tracing his lips in her mind—and her question was among the few she'd been truly curious about. Even before The Flood had happened the comings and goings of local law hadn't gone unnoticed. Town was too small and gossip was too fast, so news that Kenneth Gray had left the department and law enforcement a year after his wife had been killed had made its way through Kelby Creek with relative ease. But, why he'd chosen to come back to the department to work? That, Willa had no clue about.

Kenneth let out a little breath.

"I guess for that reason, and why you didn't come to the department right after finding the box. I couldn't stand the idea that the corruption could have leaked into our closed cases and may have been why some of our unsolved cases are still unsolved." He smiled, but it didn't reach his eyes. "Plus, Detective Lovett and Sheriff Chamblin sure made a good speech about why I was the perfect match for the job. I guess that also helped me along to agree to come back."

"And why are you the perfect match?"

Kenneth's smile wavered then faded. Tension crept into his shoulders.

She responded to the change, shifting the sleeping Delilah on her lap. Willa had hit a nerve.

"Because in all of my years in law enforcement, as a deputy and as a detective, I only ever gave up on one case."

He didn't explain further.

He didn't need to.

Willa chose her next words with care.

"I don't think men like you give up, Detective. Even if they themselves think they have."

Kenneth didn't look like he believed what she'd said but he didn't dispute it. He changed the subject and tapped his open notebook.

"I'm officially taking on Josiah's case tomorrow when I get to work. That really boils down to me telling the sheriff that I'm focusing on looking into what happened to him, seeing if Leonard Bartow took the cloth from the box, and why, and then going through the rest of contents in the box."

Willa tried not to get excited but she made a little squeak.

He jabbed at his notes again and kept a stern expression. "I've already started by calling Mae's brother this morning who, like you said, didn't seem that pleased to be called. But he did give me a rundown of what happened that day as he knew it, which wasn't much. He didn't seem to be close to Josiah or Mae and, since the kids were placed into foster care after he declined becoming their guardian, we can't track them down. As for other family, you were right. There doesn't seem to be anyone else. At least anyone we can find."

Willa's heart squeezed at that. Kenneth continued.

"But next I'll start with the gun to see if I can't follow the serial number and chain of sale somewhere. *But* if I can't, or if it's not connected to Josiah at all, and we don't find any actual evidence suggesting foul play, I can't guarantee I'll keep looking into him. I learned enough to follow hunches as well as leads, but I can only do that for so long. Especially since I have an office at the department filled with other cases that need looking into."

Willa rocked forward in her seat, nodding with enthusiasm. She'd worn her hair down and felt it bounce around her head with the same energy. Kenneth agreeing to talk to her was different than him agreeing to treat her theory with an official tag labeling it.

It was validating.

It was exciting.

It made her stomach do a little flip, though that might have been at the way Kenneth was searching her face to see if she understood.

"That sounds like a fair plan to me."

"Good. I can swing by your place tomorrow and grab the box." He stood and Delilah popped up like a daisy, tail already wagging.

Willa was less ready to leave the office. She liked talking with Kenneth, even if the topics hadn't been the peppiest.

"Or, I could give it to you tonight? Maybe at dinner?" The words tumbled out with such speed that Willa didn't have time to blush. "I mean treating you to a meal after you saved my life yesterday is the very least I could do."

Kenneth paused, one hand on his cell phone and the other on the back of his chair. She'd caught him off guard, which was apparent enough, but beyond that, she couldn't read his expression.

"Dinner," he repeated.

Willa stood, too, as Delilah made a break for her owner.

"Yeah, just a friendly little thing. Or we could grab a drink, if you prefer. Whatever suits your fancy. I'm not picky."

Whatever hesitation had been there shuffled off.

Kenneth nodded, though there was some stiffness to it.

"I could use a good, friendly dinner."

Willa felt her smile widen at the news.

Even if she wasn't exactly happy about the friend part.

EVERYTHING WAS LOOKING UP. Not only had she been taken seriously about Josiah, she'd also decided to finally tell Martha and Kimball about the box and everything she'd found out. Willa had decided, though, that she would tell Ebony after Kenneth did what he was going to do to make it official, and then ask that everyone keep quiet so the gossip mill didn't take over.

Martha and Kimball had been hot and cold about the information when she'd sat down with them at lunchtime. They'd been intrigued and upset that they hadn't been told sooner. They had wanted to know where the ring in the box had come from as well as the gun. They'd split in their opinion on Leonard Bartow and whether or not he was just a run-of-the-mill burglar or if it had been his second attempt to find the gun. Martha thought he'd probably taken the bloody cloth the first time.

"Whose blood do we even think that belongs to?" Kimball had asked. "Josiah?"

"That's what I think," Willa had responded. "But Kenneth still isn't sure. He thinks the ring and the bullet casing are more recent than the other items. I don't think he's convinced they're even all connected."

The three of them had pondered that for a while before Kimball and her sister had gone back to work. That left Willa feeling antsy for far too long, especially left alone in her apartment. So she did what every antsy, Southern woman did when she felt she needed to do something.

She cleaned.

She dusted first, used the Lysol second, and then vacuumed. Somehow, after that, she ended up using the disinfectant again. Then her attention went to the baseboards before pulling her to the bathroom to mop, Windex and, once more, use Lysol to clean everything. She even wiped down her newly-repaired front door thanks to Kimball's friendship with a local woodworker. He'd been quick the night before and now, although it needed paint, the door shut and locked like brand new.

By the time she was done, her small apartment smelled like lemon and she had a slight headache.

She also hadn't killed enough time.

The clock built into the microwave said it was only just after three, which meant she had a few hours before her dinner engagement with Kenneth at six.

"You could read something," she said out loud to herself, feeling like she'd drunk a whole pitcher of sweet tea. She couldn't sit still. "Or you could bake."

Willa looked at the small recipe book Martha had given her for Christmas. It was sitting on the kitchen counter. Called the "Brownie Bible," it contained over fifty types of brownies made from scratch.

Did Kenneth like brownies?

Who didn't like brownies?

Sure in herself and the fact that she believed Kenneth did like them, Willa found her favorite recipe and went to see if she had all the ingredients. She wasn't all that upset when she didn't find every one of them.

Instead, it seemed like a good excuse to eat up a little more time. She changed out of the clothes she'd put on to clean in, and danced into a pair of blue jeans that did her curves some nice favors, a frilly blouse that matched her increasingly good mood, and a pair of flats, setting the old tennis shoes she'd been wearing off to the side.

She left the apartment feeling good and with a little hop in her step.

So much so, that she didn't even mind the dark cloud hanging over downtown as she pulled into a community parking lot. She threw her purse across her shoulder, decided it wasn't too much of a run from the grocery store to the car if it started to rain, and headed into the grocery store with a song in her head and a smile on her lips.

How had she gone from being so terrified the day before to feeling like she was almost floating now?

Had Kenneth really made all the difference?

She barely knew him.

Yet, there she was buying eggs and brown sugar and wondering if he liked the center pieces or the corner pieces when it came to brownies. She was partial to corner pieces, but decided she wouldn't mind sharing. She could be diplomatic like that.

The rain still hadn't arrived by the time Willa was done shopping and her mood was still flying high, so she loaded her groceries into her car and locked the door behind her. She was on Main Street but there were shops along the parallel streets that had become a lot more interesting in the last year. The thought of one in particular pulled her along the sidewalk in the direction of the street behind her.

The rain cloud above wasn't on the same upbeat wavelength as Willa. Droplets started to dampen her hair, but she decided to not let that keep her down. She adapted by taking a left turn to cut through one of the short alleyways, one that was covered.

The rain stopped hitting her hair and Willa took that as a sign of good luck. She was ready to put that positive energy back out into the world.

Maybe she *was* that bubbly person everyone thought she was.

Maybe that wasn't such a bad thing.

Willa made it to the mouth of the alley on the far side,

took a step out onto the sidewalk and looked across the street to the Pet Market, wondering what kind of toy Delilah might like.

She didn't understand at first why her forward momentum changed direction back into the alleyway or pinpoint right away why her chest now hurt.

One second, she was deciding between getting a ball or a chew toy. The next, she was being dragged backward with startling speed.

"Let. Go."

It wasn't Willa who said the words but, given how deep and harsh they were, she could feel them vibrate through her skin. Then she realized what was happening. Someone was pulling her by the strap of her purse. The same purse that someone was trying to take off her now.

Willa fell between fight-or-flight and froze as she was pulled another foot back into the alley. She tried to turn around to see a face but all she saw was a closely shaved head and a hockey mask. That was enough to tip the scales.

Willa went into fight mode.

"Help!" she yelled as loudly as she could, panting against the struggle to stay on her feet. Essentially being dragged by the strap of her purse, it rubbed against her chest like a seat belt might pull in a car accident. That's how hard the man was trying to get it off of her.

"Say anything again and I'll—"

Lightning suddenly forked in the air above the Pet Market street and the rain intensified just as a boom of thunder sounded overhead.

There wasn't a storm coming, she realized. It was already there. And that meant it was going to be even more difficult for people to see or to hear her.

She was just going to have to struggle in this alleyway until this masked man decided he was done with her.

Willa slashed back at the man's face with her nails. They weren't long but they were sturdy thanks to a lifetime of vitamins her sister always insisted she take. She managed to get her index finger beneath the man's chin. Swiping up along its path, she slid it under the edge of the mask.

At such an awkward angle, she only managed one attempt to rip it off.

Something the man did not like.

He grunted and let go of Willa to keep the hockey mask from completely coming off.

Then Willa was all flight.

Chapter Eleven

Colleen Tate had been obsessed with the *Child's Play* movies. There's just something about Chucky, the little doll possessed with a serial killer's soul, that terrified and interested Willa's mother. If you were a Tate, then you'd seen all the movies. More than once. More than twice. More than any one person should see the serial killer movie about a doll.

But, like her sister, Willa had never been a fan. It wasn't so much about the plot as it was about the victims. They had the tendency to be smart, cautious, and surrounded by weapons. And yet, as soon as that doll was seen holding a knife, it was like every victim's good brain cell disappeared in a flurry of fear.

Willa had decided that if she was ever in a similar situation, she would be the one to keep her wits about her. Leonard Bartow surprise attacking her in her apartment excluded, of course. She'd never had the opportunity to get away from him.

This time, though, was different.

This time she'd broken away from her attacker with enough room to make it out onto the sidewalk.

It was only too bad that Willa finally understood why those characters in her mom's favorite movies seldom survived. For all the smarts that she believed she possessed, instead of heading to the very same pet store across the street, Willa seemed to lose all semblance of direction. Not only did she turn and run away from the store, she was also headed in the opposite direction of where her car was parked.

It was a disappointing self-discovery. A mistake she hadn't realized she'd made until the rain soaked her through and she was a good block from the alley.

Maybe he was gone.

Maybe she'd put up too much of a fuss and he'd decided she wasn't worth robbing.

A storefront was alight another block down. It belonged to a graphic artist who designed billboards for businesses in the county. Willa had met her once though she doubted the woman would remember her.

She definitely would after Willa barged in. "Lock the doors" is what Willa would yell first, followed by "Call 9-1-1."

But just as the rest of her life this past week hadn't gone to plan, that one, too, didn't last long.

Once again Willa was abruptly yanked backward. She didn't have time to scream. The rain pounded around her, along with her heart, as she tried to replicate the same defense she had used with the attacker the first time.

But instead of him tugging and pulling her deeper into the alleyway, the movement stopped altogether.

"Willa, it's me," came a deep voice. It was unlike the last.

Willa turned and wiped at the rain collecting on her eyelashes. The man was wearing dark jeans and a gray shirt that was just as soaked as hers. More important, he wasn't wearing a mask.

He was also Kenneth.

A fact that should have put her at ease. But Willa was starting to go numb. Fear or shock? Disbelief that within two days she been attacked by two different men?

Overwhelmed and afraid.

That's what she decided as Kenneth pulled her to him before pushing her up against the brick wall of one of the buildings. There was no overhang to this alley and it was hard to make out his face as the rain picked up. But then he bent over her and angled his chin down, and Willa understood what he was doing.

He was hiding her.

And he wasn't alone. A weight pressed against Willa's leg. Delilah was leaning against her.

Willa felt the comfort of both though it didn't last long.

The unmistakable sound of someone frustrated and running was coming upon them from the sidewalk Willa had just been pulled from. Heavy footfalls pounded the pavement, the sound much louder than it would have normally been thanks to the gathering water.

The man had followed her.

Kenneth leaned in closer, making a cage out of his body around Willa. From the sidewalk, she would be hard to see.

"Does he have a gun or a knife?" Kenneth's breath brushed against her ear. Had it been a different situation, she would've shivered at the contact.

She placed her cheek against his and whispered back to him. "I—I don't know."

Kenneth nodded, moving her head as he did so, to let her know he'd heard her.

The pounding footsteps passed their alleyway.

Then Kenneth pushed something into her hand.

"Keep each other safe."

He was off and running before Willa saw that she was holding Delilah's leash.

IT HAD BEEN a long time since Kenneth had made his rounds downtown in Kelby Creek, but he didn't need to know the exact layout or where he was on the map to do what needed to be done next. Not when he had his sights on a man running full-speed away from him, donning a white mask.

"Stop! Sheriff's department!"

Kenneth's warnings did nothing. Not that he thought they would.

It had only been by chance that, while walking Delilah from the small dog park to his car, he'd seen Willa running on the opposite side of the street.

The rain had made it difficult to decipher what, exactly, had been going on until he'd noticed the way she'd been running. It hadn't been the jog of a woman who'd forgotten her umbrella or was trying to find shelter from the weather. It had been the sprint of a frightened woman. Then he'd seen the man exit the alleyway and hesitate, looking both ways.

That's all Kenneth had needed. He'd run after Willa and cut through another alley on the next block so he could grab her. He didn't know if she was hurt, or if the man who was interested in her had a weapon, or where she was going.

But he hadn't wanted to chance that she would disappear into the rainfall. Catching her had become his main priority.

Catching her attacker became his second.

Kenneth ran through the rain in the direction Willa had been headed, noting, in the distance, the lighted storefront of a local business. His leg muscles burned as he tilted forward.

The moment he'd seen Willa, he'd wished he had his gun. Just as he now wished he had his badge. But he'd been taking Delilah out for a run at the park and hadn't thought to take either. If he ran into the man, he'd have to get creative.

And physical.

Thunder clapped overhead. The small chance of rain had turned into an active thunderstorm. The booming rattled the window of the lighted graphic artist business as he slowed to look around. A short awning gave him a small respite from the rain. Through the window, two desks could be seen at the back of the front room. The lights might have been on but there was no one at either.

Kenneth ran a hand over his face, shucking off water as he tried to figure out what to do next.

If he hadn't caught up to the man, there was a good

chance he wouldn't now. The rain was only falling harder, the world around him getting darker. He was unarmed and, even though he had faith in Willa and her ability to find a safe place with Delilah to call the department, Kenneth couldn't get past the thought that if he didn't know where the man was in front of him, who was to say he hadn't doubled back and gotten behind him?

Kenneth didn't like that idea.

He made up his mind.

He would get back to Willa and wait for backup.

A man materialized out of the blanket of rain beyond the awning's cover and rammed into Kenneth like a defensive tackle going for the quarterback. A power move that gave neither man the chance to stay upright. Kenneth felt the air leave his lungs just as their combined weight propelled them right into the storefront window.

The best thing Kenneth could do in between the hit and the crash was to tuck his face into his biceps and hope the glass held.

It didn't.

Kenneth felt only the smallest resistance before momentum carried them right on through the window.

A woman screamed in the background.

Pain and adrenaline pulsed through Kenneth as he slid a few feet across tile and glass. Later, he'd marvel at how hard the hit had had to be for them to travel so far into the store, but when everything stopped moving, he knew it wasn't going to be good for him if he didn't get up quickly.

The man had the same idea.

Kenneth clocked his attacker as the man got to his feet while Kenneth tried to do the same.

The hit, the glass, the floor… It had done a number on him. Rising wasn't such an easy task.

"Dawn County Sheriff's Department," Kenneth yelled, pushing himself up and around so he was facing his attacker. He didn't mind the blood on the floor. It was most likely from both of them.

The man was wearing a hockey mask. White. It was wet and gleamed beneath the fluorescent lights of the room they were in.

Kenneth didn't like masks. Ski masks he had dealt with in his career. Protective masks for roadwork or yardwork, he could reason out.

But hockey masks? Halloween masks? Faceless things made to hide an identity in no memorable or extraordinary way?

Kenneth didn't like those.

Not since a witness had seen a man in a mask running away from Ally's body.

A nondescript mask the witness had said looked like it came from a costume, though which one, she didn't know.

It wasn't the same as the hockey mask in front of him, but to Kenneth's heart, it didn't matter.

The mask was hiding malice and violence.

Malice and violence intended for Willa and now him.

The attacker got to his feet before Kenneth could steady himself. Instead of trying to brace for another tackle or to ready his own attack, Kenneth decided if the man was going to play dirty, so was he.

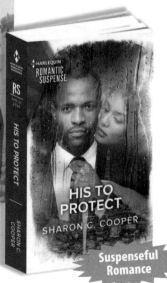

Get up to 4 FREE FABULOUS BOOKS You Love!

To thank you for being a loyal reader we'd like to send you up to 4 FREE BOOKS, absolutely free.

Just write "YES" on the Loyal Reader Voucher and we'll send you up to 4 Free Books and Free Mystery Gifts, altogether worth over $20, as a way of saying thank you for being a loyal reader.

Try **Harlequin® Romantic Suspense** books featuring heart-racing page-turners with unexpected plot twists and irresistible chemistry that will keep you guessing to the very end.

Try **Harlequin Intrigue® Larger-Print** books featuring action-packed stories that will keep you on the edge of your seat. Solve the crime and deliver justice at all costs.

Or **TRY BOTH!**

We are so glad you love the books as much as we do and can't wait to send you great new books.

So don't miss out, return your Loyal Reader Voucher Today!

Pam Powers

LOYAL READER
FREE BOOKS VOUCHER

YES! I Love Reading, please send me up to 4 FREE BOOKS and Free Mystery Gifts from the series I select.

Just write in "YES" on the dotted line below then return this card today and we'll send your free books & gifts asap!

➡️ _ YES _ _ ⬅️

Which do you prefer?

| ☐ **Harlequin® Romantic Suspense** 240/340 HDL GRHP | ☐ **Harlequin Intrigue® Larger-Print** 199/399 HDL GRHP | ☐ **BOTH** 240/340 & 199/399 HDL GRHZ |

FIRST NAME   LAST NAME

ADDRESS

APT.#   CITY

STATE/PROV.   ZIP/POSTAL CODE

EMAIL ☐ Please check this box if you would like to receive newsletters and promotional emails from Harlequin Enterprises ULC and its affiliates. You can unsubscribe anytime.

HI/HRS-520-LR21

He dove to the right, knee smashing into the tiled floor, and grabbed something they'd bowled over when they'd come through the window.

It was only after it was in his hand that Kenneth realized he was wielding an oversize closed umbrella.

Perfect.

The man missed hitting Kenneth after the dive and both turned back to each other at the same time. Kenneth couldn't help but smirk at his new weapon, brandishing it like a baseball bat.

Since this wasn't a gentleman's duel, he wasn't about to wait for a countdown to strike.

Kenneth stood to his full height and wound the umbrella in an arc behind him before swinging it at the man with all his might.

Now it was he who wasn't ready.

The umbrella hit the man's shoulder so hard that he stumbled. Kenneth brought it up and was about to go for another wind-up to strike again when the masked man showed his own weapon of choice.

Kenneth hated to admit it was a good one.

He flashed the gun's muzzle and Kenneth jumped to the side as a shot went off. Another scream sounded in the distance. Thunder backing it up a second later.

Kenneth slung his body into his attacker's, ready to keep the distance so close that the man couldn't get a good shot off again.

He'd miscalculated the man's true brazenness.

The next shot was so close to Kenneth's head, he howled, certain his eardrum exploded at the sound.

On reflex, one hand went to cup his ear while the

other grabbed for the shooter's wrist. He connected with both.

Then Kenneth was in a game of pure strength. He'd put every ounce of it into crushing the man's arm so he'd release the gun. If he could do that, he could turn the tables on the fight.

Because he didn't want to die here.

He didn't want to die at all.

Kenneth thought of Ally, his parents, the cold cases unsolved in his office.

He thought of Willa in the rain, terrified, Delilah at her side.

Kenneth pushed his other hand against the man while the one around his wrist became an unforgiving vise.

His ears were ringing but Kenneth knew the man had to let out a yell of pain.

Because right after, the gun fell to the ground.

Kenneth wasted no time. He kicked the weapon with his heel far away from both of them. Then he closed the distance between them. Using his grip, he half slung, half pushed the man to the side.

Then Kenneth turned on his heel and ran toward the gun he'd kicked away. He managed to scoop it up before it stopped moving.

He knew it was loaded due to its weight and turned around to face the man to let him know he meant business.

The man, however, wasn't just standing around. He was at the door, about to head back out into the rain.

"Stop or I'll shoot!" Kenneth commanded. His voice

sounded distorted. Maybe his eardrum had ruptured after all.

The man in the mask moved his head, as if to look at someone behind Kenneth.

It could have been a trick but Kenneth heard footsteps.

Did his attacker have a friend?

Kenneth moved with a speed he knew was only draining away and readied to defend himself against the new threat.

And it was in that moment that Kenneth knew the man in the mask would get away. That he would let him run out into the rain and disappear.

And the man in the mask knew that, too.

Because it wasn't a friend or a partner who had shuffled up to their fight.

It was a woman in tears.

A woman holding her stomach as a gunshot wound bled out into her blouse.

Kenneth got to her just as she fell to the ground, softening the blow before she hit the tile. He kept the gun in his hand and readjusted his aim toward the door again.

It was open, the sound of rain uncaring and loud.

The man was gone.

Chapter Twelve

Haven Hospital was small and the only hospital within the town limits. It was privately owned and therefore impeccably kept. It was also surprisingly modern. White, clean hallways. Private rooms that looked like they could belong in a hotel. A cafeteria with food that wasn't just convenient for the staff but actually desired.

It was all a nice picture.

Professional. Reliable. Comforting.

It didn't at all match with how Kenneth looked when Willa finally found him.

"He's okay, right?" she'd asked the nurse, a friend of her sister's named Janelle.

"Physically, yes. He had some wicked cuts but nothing some cleaning and bandaging couldn't fix. He also is going to need to take some pain pills for his shoulder I suspect, but the doctor will run that down for him when he gets back."

Willa hadn't questioned the emphasis on *physically* or the need to specify until she was standing on the other side of a hospital bed from the man.

He was in a chair next to it, elbows resting on the

sheets, hands held together. His eyes took their time rising from them up to her.

Willa's heart squeezed and then squeezed even tighter.

"Oh, Kenneth."

Blood stained his shirt in an awful pattern and bandages covered spots on his arms.

But it was his red eyes and empty hands that made Willa nearly weep.

"Oh, Kenneth," she repeated, hurrying to his side. "I'm so sorry, honey."

Willa knelt beside his chair and didn't for a moment think about personal space. She slipped between his knees and the hospital bed and put her body against his until he molded around her, accepting her embrace. There wasn't enough room for her to hug him at such an awkward angle so she settled on his lap. The side of her body was flush against him. If they had been standing he would have been holding her like a husband taking his bride over the threshold. But that wasn't the case now. Willa put her arms around him and her face into the crook of his neck.

She would have never embraced someone so intimately in any other situation but, for now, it was simple.

She wanted Kenneth to know she was there.

For him.

With him.

And he didn't seem to mind. It took a moment but his arms wound around her waist as he supported her against him. Then his head went down into her hair.

The last time they'd been close—but not *this* close—Willa had been sobbing while Kenneth had remained still.

This time, neither said or did a thing.

Kenneth let her hold him and that was enough.

They stayed like that for several minutes until finally he let out a long, ragged breath.

Willa pulled back and knew their time was done. She took his chin in her hand, looked him square in the eye and knew he'd cried. Or had tried hard not to. It was all so heartbreaking, but there wasn't anything Willa could do to assuage that break. Instead, she tilted his chin so she could kiss his cheek.

Then she untangled herself from the man and stood.

Because she wasn't a fan of hospitals—who was in this town?—and Kenneth made no indication he was going to move, Willa took a small chair from the corner and positioned it on the other side of the hospital bed. It gave her a clear view of the detective and his brilliant eyes of dark, deep water staring right at her.

She wanted to give him space—because wasn't that what you were supposed to do in situations like this?—but that wasn't who she was.

And what had happened wasn't something silence could heal.

Plus, Willa hadn't seen him since their run-in in the alleyway in the rain. After that she'd gone to the Pet Market with Delilah and called in the department. She'd waited there until sirens filled downtown.

The rain hadn't let up but Willa had been readying to venture out when a firetruck and ambulance flew past. But Deputy Carlos Park had showed up for her first.

"Detective Gray sent me," he'd said. There was such a mass hesitation that Willa knew something had happened. That something was wrong. Even when the deputy had assured her that Kenneth was all right.

It had been a few hours since she'd had that conversation with Deputy Park and those hours had felt excruciating not being able to see Kenneth or to talk to him. Though she understood why.

Kenneth had resumed placing his hands on the bed between them. He gave them another long look before meeting her gaze again. For the first time since everything had happened, Willa thought he seemed to acknowledge that a significant passage of time had indeed passed. At least, it felt significant to her.

"I'm sorry I didn't call…" he started. His voice was a little hoarse. He'd been yelling. But why and at who, she could only guess for the moment. "Deputy Park said he had you and you were okay."

"I was," Willa confirmed. "Delilah, too."

That stirred him a bit more. "Is she here?"

Willa shook her head.

"She's with Martha and Kimball at the house. Don't worry, though, they're great with dogs and said they're more than happy to watch her until you're ready. I also remembered seeing the bag of dog food at your house when I was there this morning, so we went ahead and got her a bag at the store. So don't you worry, she's really okay."

If it had been earlier in the day, Willa suspected that Kenneth would shake his head, thank her, and then insist on not being a burden in some gentlemanly way that he thought was right. But he didn't do that now. He simply nodded, weary.

Willa decided not to bring up that, while the law worked to contain and sift through what had happened, Willa and her sister and Kimball had worked to settle things for Kenneth. Thanks to Deputy Park, Kenneth's keys had been taken before he'd been carried off in the ambulance to the hospital. His SUV was in the parking lot downstairs and Willa's car was back at her place.

That was one of the very great things about living in a small town with a solid support system. When something bad happened, you never went through it alone, even if you didn't realize it.

Willa didn't want to seem like she was looking for a pat on the back for their resourceful accommodation or for having given some forethought to what might happen next. Instead she waited for him to speak again.

When it didn't seem like he would, Willa was gentle. "Do you need to stay here any longer?"

On the way up to his room, Willa had run into only two deputies, one of them Deputy Park. They had been heading out. Surely that meant Kenneth could leave. "Or does the doctor need you to stay?" she asked.

That got an immediate answer.

"I can leave. I'm fine." He looked down at his shirt.

Willa's heart squeezed again.

She heard what he hadn't said.

He was fine.

LeAnne Granger was not.

A stray bullet from the masked man's gun had found her and, though Kenneth had tried his best to save her before the first responders arrived, she'd died in his arms on the floor of her business. Surrounded by blood and broken glass, according to Deputy Park when Willa had finally gotten the truth from him.

"I've never had someone die in my arms," Park had commented after he'd told her, shaking his head, a pained expression lining his face. "No one should have that happen but especially not Kenneth. Not after—" The deputy had caught himself and buttoned up the conversation. Willa found it touching that he hadn't wanted to gossip about something so sensitive to Kenneth, though it wasn't hard to put together that he'd been talking about Ally Gray.

As far as Willa knew, Kenneth hadn't found Ally, but he had been called to the scene when her body had been called in.

Holding a woman, even as she died, wouldn't have been easy for anyone. But for someone whose wife had been murdered? It had to bring back memories that were a new level of unbearable.

Willa reached out and touched Kenneth's hands. It brought his attention away from a shirt he should have already taken off.

"Here. You stay put and I'll be back in a second."

He didn't make a fuss as Willa went out into the hall and searched for Janelle.

A few minutes later, she was back in the room, a clean white T-shirt in her hands. She stopped next to Kenneth's chair and took his elbow.

"Why don't we switch your shirts out?" she said,

keeping her voice soft as she tried to gently pull him up. Thankfully, Kenneth stood on his own.

He was in a daze, probably deep in his thoughts, re-playing what had happened to LeAnne or to his wife or on something else that would give Willa nightmares, but he seemed to be fine with following her directive.

In one fluid movement, he pulled his shirt up and off. Willa took it before he could focus on the dried blood again and handed him the new one.

"Where'd you get this?" he asked, pulling it over his head.

Willa hurried to the trashcan in the room and, hoping he wasn't attached to the plain gray shirt, was quick to throw it away.

"I noticed a male nurse on shift who was about your size. He had a spare in his locker," she said, scooting back to his side. "He said it was no problem if you took it since he has a ton at home."

Kenneth nodded absently.

Willa hesitated before taking the lead again.

"Is…is there anyone you want me to call? That you need to talk to?" She knew about Ally but her death had been years ago. With a burning blush, Willa realized she had no idea if the detective was attached to anyone else. Sure, there was no ring on his finger, but he could have been dating someone. So far all of their interactions had been about Josiah and the box. Just because she'd been feeling a little more than what she'd let on, didn't mean that Kenneth returned those same sentiments.

So she waited, feeling incredibly selfish for hoping that he wasn't seeing anyone, for him to answer.

He did so with little fanfare, though it struck a chord with her nonetheless.

"The only person I was planning to call was you."

He reached back to the table behind him and grabbed his phone and wallet. There was also a sheet of paper. She spied a doctor's signature at the bottom. Probably a prescription for heavy-duty ibuprofen for his shoulder, like Janelle had said. He folded the paper and slipped it into his jeans.

For the first time Willa noticed that there was some blood on there, too. Along with his shoes.

"Let's go." She put her hand on the small of his back, feeling waves of protectiveness and helplessness lap over her at the same time. They stopped at a nurses' station to make sure the paperwork was taken care of, and Willa waved goodbye to Janelle. It wasn't until they were in the parking lot that Kenneth peeked out of his own thoughts for a moment when he saw they were headed for his SUV.

"I don't have my keys." He patted his jeans.

"I do. Don't worry."

Kenneth nodded. He became quiet again.

And that's how the rest of the night went.

Willa made the decisions, Kenneth went along for the ride.

She drove him straight home and let him inside his own house before sitting him down at his dining room table. She made him a turkey sandwich, got him a water, and called her sister to make sure she could keep Delilah overnight.

When he was done eating, she guided him to the

shower and left him, to make another call to her sister. Once he'd changed, she shooed him into bed with little to no resistance.

He'd fallen asleep faster than she'd anticipated.

Willa paused by his bed in the middle of her current task of collecting his discarded clothes for the laundry and looked long and hard at the man.

She became misty-eyed at his face slack from sleep.

Good people watching bad things was no life to live. At least, no life to live alone.

THERE WAS A knock on the door. He could have cussed at the interruption. He'd already bandaged himself but had had to change it out twice already. The first had bled through his shirt; the second had pulled uncomfortably.

"Honey! You'll never believe what I just heard!" His wife's voice was excited, pitched high and vibrating.

He could ruin her fun, tell her he had a good idea of what she'd just heard, but that wasn't part of his plan. So he used the voice he reserved for her and called back through his closed office door.

"I'm on a call, dear. Give me a few minutes and I'll come talk, okay?"

She wasn't a fan of that but, to his surprise, had been a good wife when it came to his privacy. If he told her to not disturb him without knocking on his office door first, she didn't. If he told her he couldn't talk right then, she waited.

Just as she did now.

"Okay. I'll be in the kitchen when you're through."

He heard her pad away and continued to check on his cuts. Then he looked at the bruise on his arm that would only get nastier.

He couldn't believe Detective Gray had hit him with an umbrella.

He also couldn't believe he'd left his gun behind.

As for the woman who had been shot by accident...

Well, nothing he could do about that now.

So he finished up and thought about his options. He became angry and then he cooled.

He was the smart one.

The patient one.

Then why did you attack the detective? You could have just let him go.

It was a question that had been bothering him since he'd escaped.

But one impulsive decision wasn't going to affect him. He wouldn't let it.

Impulsive or not, patient or not, there was somewhere else that he needed to be. Something he needed to fix.

Because that's what he did.

He fixed mistakes, especially ones that others made.

And, boy, was there one he needed to fix sooner rather than later.

For now, he checked that his shirt covered his injuries, was thankful for that bit of good luck, and left the office for his kitchen.

His wife was on him in seconds.

"That woman who got shot? The Granger lady? She died! Isn't that awful?"

She grabbed his hand and squeezed.
He squeezed it back.
"That *is* awful, isn't it?"

Chapter Thirteen

Light splayed across the foot of the bed. Kenneth blinked away sleep and took in the sight slowly.

He looked down at his hands and got lost for a moment.

His alarm went off after that. A series of chirps on his phone that annoyed him to no end, especially since he always seemed to wake a minute or two before it. He rolled over and slapped at his phone on the nightstand, dismissing it.

Then he saw the charging chord attached to it.

Kenneth tried to think back to the night before. Plugging in his phone was always the last thing he did before sleep, but he knew for a fact he hadn't done it last night. In fact, he'd lost track of his phone entirely somewhere between food and his shower.

Kenneth sat up, ramrod-straight.

Willa.

He looked around his room, expanding his attention to detail.

A pair of jeans sat folded on top of his dresser. He

got out of bed, walked through the pain in his shoulder that made him wince, and held up the jeans.

They were clean.

So were his shoes, sitting stain-free on the floor next to him.

His gray shirt, however, was nowhere to be found.

That didn't surprise him. Not after—

The sound of dishes clattering together pulled Kenneth's attention again. When he opened his bedroom door and walked out into the hallway, he could smell something that made his mouth instantly water. He followed it out and down the stairs to the kitchen, minding the pain as he took each step.

Kenneth turned the corner and saw sunshine in his kitchen.

Sunshine trying to reach a plate on a shelf too high for her.

"Let me."

Willa whirled around, hand going to her chest.

"Kenneth!"

The day before felt like a lifetime ago but Kenneth knew Willa had changed from the outfit he'd seen soaked through in the alley and then again in their quiet conversation at the hospital. She was casually dressed, with her hair down, framing her face, and jeans and a light blue blouse that clung more than it flowed. There were no shoes on her feet but there was a pair of socks. They were pink and had hearts all over them. Cute was the word that came to mind for them.

Beautiful was the word that came to mind for her.

"I didn't hear you moving around," she added after

his quick look up and down her body. Her cheeks took on a rosier hue. Then her eyes widened, her brows knitting together. "I didn't wake you, did I?"

Kenneth shook his head and went for the items she'd been trying to reach. With effort, he hid how it hurt to grab plates and bring them down.

"I always wake up around now," he assured her. "I think it's part of my DNA at this point."

Willa took the plates from him and waved him to the doorway that led into the dining room.

"Well, now that you're up, let's go ahead and eat. I hope you like bacon and cinnamon rolls because that's all we have."

Kenneth told her that he did and soon they were seated at the small table, each with food that smelled delicious, and a pot of coffee.

Everything had all happened so fast that Kenneth hadn't thought to question any of it until he was one cinnamon roll deep. He supposed he must have been hungrier than he'd thought.

"I didn't know I had cinnamon rolls. Or bacon, for that matter."

Willa looked up from her food and smiled.

"You didn't. Actually, you didn't really have anything, but Martha is a ridiculously early riser and offered to bring some of each over. She baked the rolls and the bacon. She's big into breakfast." Willa averted her eyes and grinned. "I guess I should have opened with that instead of hoping you'd thought I was the one who went through the trouble of making them."

Kenneth shook his head.

"Hey, if it had been just me, I would have had the coffee and saved a buck fifty for the vending machine at work. This—" he motioned to his plate "—is much appreciated, whether you physically made it or not."

Willa seemed cheered by that. Her smile widened. "Well, for what it's worth, I do make a mean everything-in-it omelet."

He believed her. "I'll have to try it sometime."

They lapsed into a silence while they finished their food. It wasn't like the night before when Kenneth had locked himself in his own head. This time he was trying to backtrack, to see outside his thoughts about Le-Anne and the hockey-masked man.

Kenneth had made it home, in a new shirt, been fed, directed to the shower, and told to go to sleep. He'd had his clothes washed, his phone charged, and had been served breakfast.

And all because of Willa.

"I wanted—"

"Willa—"

Both spoke at the same time and both stopped.

Willa's face tinted pink.

Kenneth chuckled. "You go first," he said.

Willa obliged.

"I just wanted to say I hope I didn't overstep by staying here last night. Or by invading your privacy and making some decisions without your input." She got up and walked over to where her purse was sitting on a chair that seemed to collect junk mail.

Willa fished inside it until she pulled out a keyring. It

and the keys belonged to him. She set them down next to him on the table and took her seat again.

"For instance, driving your car around without your consent and for also letting Martha and Kimball keep Delilah overnight when you don't even know them. And, well again, staying here after you'd gone to sleep." She shifted in her seat, outwardly uncomfortable. "I just didn't want you to be alone is all, and thought I could help. I hope you're not too mad or think I'm a loon."

Kenneth didn't have to think about what to say. It came out with a smile he hoped she realized was genuine.

"I was going to thank you, Willa." She gave him an apprehensive look. "I mean it." He tried to drive his appreciation home. "Last night was hard. You didn't have to help but you did. You made everything a little less…" Kenneth couldn't find the right word. He let it lie and reiterated his first point. "What I'm saying is thank you. I mean it."

Willa tucked her chin a little. She was back to smiling. It was small but sincere. But then it faded.

He knew what came next.

"I'm the one who should be thanking *you*." Her hand fisted around the handle of her coffee mug. "And apologize again. If you hadn't grabbed me when you had, that man would have caught me, I'm sure of it." A shadow passed over her face. "But if I had run the right way or if I had been more aware of my surroundings, Le-Anne…you… None of this would have—"

"No." Kenneth's voice was pure force. It made Willa's gaze snap up to his in a flash. "This isn't your fault.

Not one ounce of any of it. Not LeAnne's death. Not me getting hurt. Not even him trying to take your bag. The only person to blame is the person who actually did every single one of those things. You got it? Willa?"

She sniffled, surprising him that she'd been so close to tears, but nodded. There she had been, helping him while also riddled with self-imposed guilt.

A feeling Kenneth knew all too well.

He softened again. "It's a hard lesson," he admitted. "Easier said than done, too."

"Then let me remind *you* that LeAnne's death isn't your fault, either. It was that man's. You did everything you could to save her."

Kenneth couldn't help but look at his hands. After he'd called for help, he'd tried to use them to stop the bleeding. But the lone bullet had done too much damage. He'd lost a heartbeat before the EMTs had arrived. Still, he'd gone with her to the hospital, tied to her in death since he'd been the one to face it with her.

The way she'd looked up at him before she'd gone…

Kenneth could feel it pulling him back into himself again. Just as it had last night.

"You can talk about it, if you want." Willa's voice was small but strong.

Kenneth didn't want to talk about it. Yet he did.

"I've seen death before on the job. Some things I've tried very hard to forget and other memories sneak up on me sometimes. But last night was the first time I'd seen anything like that since Ally passed." His felt his jaw harden. "I knew LeAnne wasn't going to make it and, when you can't save someone, the best you can do is be there with them—really be there—at their end. To see them out of this world with compassion and attention."

Kenneth shook his head slowly. His eyes found the sunshine across the table from him. He felt shame. Deep and cutting.

"But I couldn't even give LeAnne that," he said. "I knew she was going, but when I looked down at her, all I could think about was Ally."

He hadn't wanted to tell anyone that truth. In fact, he'd planned to bury it so deep within himself that it would only haunt his nightmares.

There was something about Willa, though. Something that made him feel comfortable and able to give in enough to show her that he valued her presence.

He valued *her.*

Kenneth thumbed the spot where his wedding band had once sat on his ring finger.

"I don't know how much you've heard about what happened to my late wife, but she was killed and left out in a field. Shot. Like LeAnne. But alone. No one with her as she bled out. Just her and the grass and the sun overhead."

He took a breath. The ache that never went away sent a pulse of fresh pain through him. "Holding LeAnne, seeing her like that… All I could think about was if that was how it had happened with Ally. If she'd tried to stop the bleeding, hoped someone would save her. Or if she'd known there was no hope and given up out there. Closed her eyes and then never opened them again. All alone. And I hate that. I hate that I couldn't give LeAnne the focus she deserved. I couldn't save her and I couldn't get out of my own head to say goodbye to her."

That was it, he realized. That was why he'd gone into his head after he'd seen LeAnne was shot. That was why he'd operated on reflex and muscle memory.

It was why he'd let Willa take over.

That, and because he trusted her.

No small feat, he reckoned, but didn't have the head-space to think more on just yet.

He watched Willa push back her chair and come to his side. She took his chin in her hand as she had the night before in the hospital. Instead of kissing his cheek, she bent her head. Her lips were soft and warm and quick against his.

When she broke the brief kiss, her cheeks had gone rosy again.

"If I'm keeping count, that's the third time you've kissed me," Kenneth found himself saying. The world didn't totally feel real at the moment, caught between a nightmare and a dream.

Willa let his face go but held his attention like she was a bright, stunning flame and he was a moth with a mighty need for light.

"I should apologize for that, too, but I won't." She held up three fingers and ticked off each point as she made one. "The first kiss was because I needed com-fort. The second one was because you needed comfort. This one, the third, was only for the fact that you're a good, good man, Kenneth Gray, and I don't want you to ever think otherwise. You got that?"

Her lips had been soft. Her tone now was not.

She meant what she said.

And she wanted an answer from him. No smart-alecky remarks and no backtalk.

So he didn't give her either.

"Yes, ma'am."

Willa nodded, straightening. She smoothed her shirt down and tossed some of the hair that had fallen over her shoulder at her earlier movement across her back again.

"Good," she said simply. "If you need more reminding that none of this is your fault, just let me know and I'll kiss you quiet again."

Kenneth could tell she hadn't meant to say that by the way she paused and her cheeks turned a darker shade of crimson, but he laughed all the same.

"I'll keep that in mind."

She nodded again and was off with their dishes into the kitchen.

Kenneth went back to his bathroom to get ready and change.

After giving the office a quick call, he made his way to the living room. A folded blanket sat on the couch's end, a pillow on top. She'd slept on the couch.

Because she hadn't wanted him to be alone.

Kenneth cleared his throat as Willa joined him in the living room.

She looked expectantly at him. "It's not a coincidence, is it?" she asked. "Leonard Bartow happens to break into my apartment, the bloody cloth goes missing, and then a man tries to take my purse or me two days later."

Kenneth didn't think so. Not at all.

He said as much.

"I think it's all connected." He sighed. "We just don't know how yet."

Willa pushed her shoulders back, determination hardening her usually soft features. "Then what can we do now?"

Kenneth could already feel his anger rising.

She shouldn't be a part of this, but there Willa was, right in the center it seemed.

How he wished she wasn't.

Kenneth locked his eyes with hers and hoped she felt every vestige of intent behind his next words.

"Now, we fight back until this entire thing is over."

Chapter Fourteen

They should have known that, at some point, living in a small town would have unforeseen complications. What they hadn't expected, though, was that they get two steps into the sheriff's department's lobby on a Friday morning and find one.

The man had a Guns N' Roses tattoo on his forearm and anger in his eyes. He lunged at Kenneth before anyone could stop him. Willa, tucked at the detective's side, didn't see what was happening until Kenneth moved to become a wall in front of her. His protection cost him a right hook to the jaw.

A deputy and two civilians in the lobby jumped up to step in. They separated the men enough to get the story behind the attack.

The man who had delivered the hit was Jason Whitmore, LeAnne Granger's fiancé.

And he was grieving.

"I've been there before," Kenneth told Willa after assuring her for the umpteenth time within the span of a few minutes that he was okay.

He'd smiled; it was strained to the max. "We picked

up my pain meds for my arm. They'll help my face, too." He'd looked over at the still-riled-up Jason. "I need to talk to him. Why don't you go get started on filling in Detective Lovett while I do that?"

Willa had agreed and was escorted to the lead detective's office by Deputy Kathryn Juliet. They'd gone to school together but hadn't been more than acquaintances. Still, Juliet, as she'd told everyone to call her growing up, said she was glad that Willa was okay.

It had been a nice sentiment and Willa thanked her for it.

Then she was looking at Foster Lovett, another local. Though, he had left the fold with his high school sweetheart only to come back years later, divorced but accomplished. He'd been the first new hire to really make a difference, according to Martha and Ebony's opinions, in the department since its name and reputation had been tainted. The job suited him, as had his experience. Because of them, he was well-liked, had gotten married and, most recently, had become a father.

"Willa Tate." His smile was weary. Everyone's seemed to be lately. But maybe that was Willa's own mood projection. It didn't stop her from being polite.

"Foster Lovett, the man who returned."

He came around the desk and bypassed a congenial handshake. His hug of greeting was quick but proper. When he stepped away, he chuckled. "Hey, I heard you'd left, too."

He motioned to the chair across from his desk. Willa noted a framed picture next to the nameplate on the desktop. It was his wedding picture. It was nice.

"I went to college," she said when he'd settled back into his chair. "I'm not sure that's the same thing as going across country for a decade."

He ran a hand through his long hair. "You say it like that and I just feel old all the way to my bones."

"Don't feel too old. I'm only a few years behind you in age. Making *me* feel anything other than young and relevant would be impolite."

He snorted and held up a hand in defense. "Well, I don't want to be impolite. Not when your sister is still in town. She'd never let me hear the end of it."

The only reason Willa was friendly, or at least had been before Foster had run off, was that he'd been actual friends with Martha. Along with his ex-wife. Though Willa decided not to bring any of that up.

She wasn't there for a social call, after all.

Foster seemed to remind himself of the same thing.

He leaned forward in his chair. Something all detectives apparently did when things became serious.

"I talked to Kenneth this morning, briefly, on the phone. He said that he believes the break-in with Leonard Bartow and the attack on you downtown yesterday are connected. But we've designed the cold case unit to act independently from active cases, so I'm afraid I'm out of the loop. Bring me up to speed, if you don't mind?"

Willa didn't.

Like she had done with Kenneth, she told the detective everything. Even about the gun, which Kenneth had brought in, along with the box.

Foster didn't take notes but his eyebrows stayed furrowed as he listened. When Willa tied up the story, his look of concentration was still there. Though his gaze had shifted to the doorway.

Kenneth stood within it, the side of his face red. "What do you think?" he asked Foster.

Willa noted his hand was fisted at his side. Whatever conversation he'd had with Jason hadn't been a fun one.

"I think that, if it was anywhere other than Kelby Creek, we'd need more to go on to call this a web instead of several different non-connecting threads." He shrugged. "But this *is* Kelby Creek and, from experience, I can tell you that it may be small but it has a knack for finding a way to be a massive pain in the backside."

He gave Kenneth a questioning look. "That is why I'm going to make an executive decision for our sheriff, who's out dealing with press and the mayor, to keep you in charge of this. So what do *you* want to do? What do you need from me?"

Willa could tell Kenneth hadn't expected that. He did, however, have an answer ready.

"I want to address anyone who isn't actively patrolling or on a case. Now."

Foster nodded, not at all offended by the command. He stood. "Then let's get to it."

Willa thought she would stay in Foster's office or be taken to Kenneth's, but instead she was led to a large room filed with tables, chairs and a whiteboard.

"I hope you don't mind, but I'm going to ask you to tell your story one last time," Kenneth said to her as staff who were available started to file in a few minutes later.

Willa's stomach fluttered with nerves but she told him she didn't mind.

That lie turned into more nervous twitches as the door closed behind the last person to attend the impromptu briefing. There were almost twenty people inside the room.

Kenneth started the meeting off.

With an absolute bang.

"MY NAME IS Kenneth Gray, but a lot of you know me as the man who left this department several years ago after my wife, Ally, was shot dead in a field."

The room fell into an absolute hush. Kenneth knew without looking at her next to him that Willa's eyes had widened in shock.

He wanted to tell her he was shocked too at how bluntly he'd said it.

After speaking with Jason Whitmore, something in Kenneth had snapped. Or maybe exploded. Whatever the action, its force was still propelling him now.

At first, Kenneth hadn't known exactly what he was going to say. But he had known it wouldn't be the pep talk about catching bad guys that everyone might have expected. Nor would it be a meeting with a summary of what had happened so far. It certainly wouldn't be the cry for help that he himself had expected.

He'd known that from the moment Detective Lovett had asked him what he'd needed.

Because what he needed wasn't just something he could do on his own.

"For those who don't know that about me, know that I left the department because I couldn't find one lead, not one, in her murder," he continued. "Other men, or women, might have stayed to put more good out into the world, but I wasn't one of them. *But* then, as we know, The Flood happened and the damage from it was enough to get me back."

Kenneth paused, but not for dramatic effect. Instead he searched the faces of the men and women looking at him. He decided that he knew what needed to happen next.

"Raise your hand if you were hired or transferred in after The Flood took place."

To his surprise, six people raised their hands.

"Raise your hand if you were hired or transferred in a year or two before The Flood took place."

More hands went into the air than before.

"And raise your hand if you were heavily investigated by the FBI task forces that came in after The Flood to root out corruption because you had been here for a good chunk of time before it happened."

No one raised a hand.

Not even Detective Lovett. He had been a new hire after The Flood, despite being a local.

Kenneth raised his own hand.

He could see the surprise on some of his audience's faces. He'd never told anyone that and, as far as he knew, the interim sheriff was the only one in the department who knew. Even Lovett couldn't hide his sudden curiosity.

He lowered his hand, knowing he now had everyone's full attention.

And that was good because he had a point to make.

"Everyone knows the story. You've heard it from the gossip mill, the news, and maybe some who were directly affected. But let me make it clear exactly what happened."

Kenneth started to pace. All eyes were on him as he did so.

"Annie McHale, daughter to the beloved and quite rich McHales, went missing one day," he began. "If it had been anyone else, the reaction wouldn't have been as swift, but the McHales were a special family. Humble, compassionate, and powerful. Everyone loved and respected them, and that love and respect trickled down to Annie…

"So when a ransom call came in, it wasn't just a family worried about her. It was a whole town ready to fight. But that's not exactly how a ransom demand works. You can't have an entire town in on it without putting the very person you're trying to rescue in more danger. So the McHales turned to their best friend, and godfather to Annie. The sheriff at the time. He decided to handle the swap—five-hundred thousand dollars for Annie."

He paused again, the memory of seeing what had happened next on TV popping into his mind. As well as the memory of hearing it from his neighbor, who'd yelled at the news when her friend had called after witnessing it in person.

"We all know what happened next. There was an ambush by the kidnappers. It became a bloodbath in the park and five people were killed, several were wounded, and Annie McHale was never seen. The kidnappers managed to get away and Kelby Creek made national news because they'd hacked into the town's web site and played a live video of Annie, beaten and bloodied, begging to be saved while a kidnapper asked for a million dollars in three days or she would die."

Several people in the room seemed to physically readjust how they were sitting at that, as if trying to move away from the ugliness of the past. While the video had been taken down, it had been online long enough for recordings to be made and saved. Kenneth wouldn't doubt that everyone in Kelby Creek had seen the video at this point.

"The first FBI agents came in then to help sort everything out. One of them, Jacqueline Ortega, was the first of the two to have a hunch and follow it. She left a message on her partner's phone and disappeared. *Then* the thunderstorm came, bringing with it a nasty flash flood. That flash flood is what sent the mayor off the road and why Ortega's partner stopped to help him. That's how he found Annie's necklace in the mayor's car, and that's when he followed his new hunch that Annie's kidnappers might not be strangers at all." Kenneth looked to Willa. She was paying rapt attention. He hated to put her on the spot, but he wanted to prove that what had happened was public knowledge. "Can you tell us what happened next as you've heard it from the news and locals, Miss Tate?"

Willa's cheeks darkened but her voice was loud and clear when she spoke.

"He was able to connect the sheriff and the mayor to the kidnappers and figure out that they had been behind it all along. The FBI sent in another team to investigate. They learned that the corruption went far back and had spread like a cancer throughout the sheriff's department and other positions of authority across town. During their investigation, several people were fired and arrested. Some disappeared." She quieted a little. "Annie McHale and Jacqueline Ortega were never found."

Kenneth nodded. She gave him a small smile then was back to watching him like the rest of the room.

"Now let me tell you what they didn't advertise in the news or through the back channels of town gossip." Kenneth rolled his shoulders. He was tense. He was antsy. He was tired of not having answers.

"When the FBI first started looking into how the corruption had infiltrated this department, they were utterly overwhelmed with what they found. I only know this because, when they came to my door, they questioned every single detail of every single case I had assisted on or helped close. Every detail. Then, when that was done, they focused on everything else. Traffic stops as a rookie. Speeding tickets. What I was doing when a shooting had taken place or when a drug bust had gone down. Where I was when my wife was killed."

Rage at that, no matter how earned the question had been, would never, ever, go away for Kenneth. To be

questioned in the home he'd shared with Ally, after tire-
lessly looking for her killer, only to fall into an obses-
sion and then a depression, had been a pain that he'd
never thought he'd feel. Yet, he'd had to power through
it to keep his name clear.

"It was only after I passed muster that one of the
agents admitted they hadn't expected so many others
to be suspicious. Never mind guilty. He also told me
he wasn't sure the town could ever recover. Or that
the department would even survive the gut job it was
going to get.

"To be honest, I think at that point I was tired and
angry and I said some things I probably shouldn't have.
Things like there were still good people in the department. In the town. That trust might have been broken
but that's the great thing about trust. You can only ever
break it or earn it back. Since it was broken, that just
meant it was time to earn it back."

Kenneth had gotten to his point, even if he'd taken,
as Willa called it, the long way around.

He kept his gaze sweeping his audience.

"But I was wrong."

Kenneth flipped the whiteboard over. He'd written a
number on it before everyone had come in. The number
wasn't exact, but it was well over one hundred. "That's
how many cases and incidents were directly affected
by the corruption the FBI and the rest of us managed to
find after The Flood. That's what this department did.
The corrupted made fools out of any of us who fought
the good fight and did it all for personal and selfish
gain. That FBI agent was right, we shouldn't even be

standing with that kind of cloud above our heads." He shook his head. Angry all over again. "And that's why the criminals in this town have become more brazen. If we can't police or catch the criminals among ourselves, what hope do we have of doing anything to them."

A few nods waved through the group. Lovett's was one of them.

"That's why I'm here, right now, in front of you." Kenneth looked at Willa. "Miss Tate, here, is going to explain how she launched her own investigation into one of our cold cases and I'll tell you how we're going to help her."

This time Willa's blush was gone. She'd seemingly lost any nerves she'd been carrying.

She was curt and quick to tell them about Josiah Linderman and the box.

Then Kenneth brought it home.

"Everyone in here is now on this case and the break-in by Leonard Bartow, as well as the attempted mugging and subsequent attack by the man in the hockey mask. But I'm going to tell you two things that you probably won't hear again in this building."

Kenneth knew he could be commanding, just by his body type alone. He could make himself seem taller and wider, and turn his face into stone, while his voice flattened and swung low. He did all of those things standing there in front of the people who would hopefully help solve several mysteries all at once. He wanted them to not only hear him, he wanted them to listen.

When he was confident they were, his voice seemed to reverberate off the walls.

"You are not to trust anyone, but most specifically anyone currently in the department or who has formerly worked for the department. The town doesn't trust us for good reason. We're going to remember that reason while we work. No stone left unturned. No one is above suspicion."

He held up two fingers to show he was at his last point. "You will tell no one outside this room what we are doing. Not spouses, not friends, not coworkers. If you question someone, you find a way to tell the truth without giving it away. Someone is out there making moves that we didn't anticipate and we couldn't stop. So, even though it's a big ask to not trust and to not talk, remember that it might be the best way to find justice for people who deserved better from this department. From us."

He didn't say their names but three immediately swam behind his eyes.

LeAnne.

Josiah.

Ally.

Kenneth turned to Willa.

He refused to add her name to the list.

"Now, come to me one by one for assignments," he barked out to the room. "We've got a job to do."

Chapter Fifteen

The gun went with one person, the ring and the box with another, someone was given Leonard Bartow, and Willa thought she heard another being assigned to shuffle through files relating to anything that had happened the year that Josiah Linderman had gone missing.

Kenneth was the head of the hunt and held the authority with sangfroid. In turn he was given the reverence that Willa believed he'd earned by his speech. Though, to say she was surprised that the speech was meant to make each person in the room not trust a soul, was an understatement.

It was also the first thing Kenneth addressed when they were alone in his office.

"Telling someone they can't trust anyone, especially during an investigation, usually makes them uncomfortable and cautious. It makes them choose their actions carefully and double-check their work. Not a long-term solution but, for now, I need everyone sharp, fast but thorough, and knowing that I'm not talking just to talk. I want this handled."

The way he spoke, with such conviction, gave Willa goose bumps.

She asked how she could help.

Kenneth checked his watch. "I need to do a few things here, but do you think you could reach out to your boss, or whoever was in charge of making the agreement to develop the land you found the box buried on? I need as much information on it and the developer as possible. Maybe if you ask about it, you'll get less scrutiny than if I send a deputy or even go myself."

Willa felt a little shame that she hadn't thought of that herself, but nodded. "I can do that."

"Good. We might not know yet who buried the box but maybe if we found out why it was buried *there*, we can follow it back to some answers."

Willa agreed. She was already thinking about the paperwork she could find herself as office manager when Kenneth announced she wasn't going alone.

"You're the common denominator in the attacks, so you're not leaving my sight until this is over." Willa might have normally scoffed at the somewhat sexist and demanding statement but there was no denying she felt relief. For more reasons than one.

She didn't want to be alone.

She didn't want Kenneth to be alone.

"I thought you didn't want anyone to know what we were doing?" She couldn't imagine Bobby Thornton, her boss and connection to the developer, wouldn't stare at Kenneth's presence when she spoke to him.

"I'll stay in the car." He held up his cell. "I can still make headway from my phone."

It took them a few minutes as Kenneth finished up, but it wasn't long before they were headed to her office.

Willa had already spoken to Bobby that morning, just as she had the day before about taking some personal days off. When she stepped through the front door solo, he came out into the small lobby with arms wide.

"Willa." His tired eyes drank her in before he was all hug. Bobby was pushing seventy but had made it a point to tell anyone who would listen that retirement was for the birds. And he wasn't a fan of flying.

He gave her a quick squeeze and then stepped back to look at her, full of concern. Along with wanting to die behind a desk instead of anywhere else, Bobby was known for his absolute love for his wife. Willa was surprised to not see her there. The very few times Willa had called off, she had come in to help out. Unlike her husband, she fully believed in relaxing after decades of working.

"How are you?" he asked, seeming to accept that, at least physically, Willa appeared to be all right. "I thought we agreed that you should take a few days. I mean, after what happened, I can barely focus on the work and I wasn't even there."

Kenneth might have been spouting the rule to not tell anyone about the investigation into Josiah and the two current attacks, but that didn't mean news of the latter hadn't already spread. Kelby Creek had been known to have the occasional uptick of excitement since The Flood but, as far as she could remember, no one had been outright killed. At least, no one innocent.

LeAnne Granger's death had changed things.

It wasn't gossip that had put the mugging turned deadly out into the town, it was facts.

A man had attacked one woman and killed another. Neither piece of news was to be taken lightly.

Willa patted Bobby's hand, still on her shoulder.

"I'm not here for the day but, you know me, always working up here." She tapped her temple with her finger and smiled. That smile was tight and a mask for the discomfort of stepping around the truth to the boss she respected. "I was thinking about a new filing system to take when we need to be on-the-go and was wondering if I could ask you a few questions about some of our current jobs. About some details I realized I didn't have. You know, to keep my focus at home instead of worrying about everything else outside of it."

Willa swore when this was all over, she'd buy Bobby a big ol' steak and apologize for her dishonesty. Until then, she was glad—and filled with guilt—when Bobby nodded and said it was a good idea.

He led her past her own office and into his, then Willa got down to business.

Twenty minutes later she was saying goodbye, telling Bobby that his wife didn't need to worry herself with bringing Willa any homemade pie, and promising to see him Monday, bright and early.

When she got into Kenneth's SUV, he was finishing up a phone call. He waited until he was done to start driving.

"Did you find anything?" he asked her in greeting.

Willa sighed.

"The name of the company who bought Lot 427,

Red Tree Development, but that was all the information we had on file. I'll have to call them and see if I can get more specific. Maybe we'll find something useful."

Willa wasn't sure of that but she had hope.

"Who was that?" she asked, turning her attention fully to him.

Kenneth was tense.

"Remember I told you that Leonard Bartow woke up but only talked long enough to get himself a lawyer?"

Willa nodded. Part of her had been glad he'd been silent. Her hope was that he'd take that silence and let it, and the evidence against him, earn him a jail cell.

"Apparently he wants to talk. To me."

That made her eyebrow pop up. "Did he say why you?"

Kenneth shook his head. "No. Just that he'll only co-operate with the man in charge of the cold case unit."

"Does he realize that man is the same one he attacked and threatened?"

"No," he said again. "I don't think so, at least. I'll find out soon."

Instead of angling the SUV in the direction of the department, she noted he'd turned in the direction of the hospital. Not her favorite place. But, after all, Leonard had been hit by a car, so it stood to reason that he was still in Haven Hospital. The thought that he'd been in the same building when Willa was with Kenneth the day before made her skin crawl.

Kenneth placed his hand on top of Willa's. His was warm. He was also sensing her unease.

"You don't have to see him. You can stay out in the

hall with the guard on duty," he assured her. "Or, if it makes you feel better, I can take you back to the department."

Willa shook her head. "I might not like the man but I want to know what he has to say."

Kenneth nodded and put his eyes back on the road.

Yet, he kept his hand right where it was until they parked at the hospital.

LEONARD BARTOW'S ATTORNEY was shaking his head as he left. Kenneth didn't blame him. He'd just been dismissed by his client in words so loud they'd reverberated through the third-floor hallway.

Willa watched him go, Kenneth watched Willa. She hadn't said a word since she'd agreed to come with him to see Bartow and now he wished she had. Kenneth couldn't tell what she was thinking. Not at the moment, at least. Other than obvious concern, there was something beneath the surface.

Something he wished they could talk about.

But now wasn't the time.

Not with Leonard ready to talk.

The hospital's security guard—the man's nametag read Billings—moved from his spot next to Leonard's hospital room door.

"He's handcuffed to the bed," he said in greeting. "But everyone's said he's been a good patient. Hasn't kicked up a fuss since I've been here, either."

"I suppose he saves that for the women he attacks," muttered Willa.

It sobered the guard.

"Yeah, that's not right." He turned to address Kenneth directly. "Between hospital security and the deputies sent our way, Mr. Bartow hasn't been alone since he was brought in. We've been on him 24/7."

"Good." Kenneth didn't think Leonard would try to pull much considering he had a broken leg and arm. But, after the week he'd had, Kenneth wasn't about to assume anything. "Willa, are you good to stay out here or—"

He watched Willa flinch and cover her ears at the same time he felt the urge to do the same. An alarm screeched throughout the hallway with awful intention.

"Is that the fire alarm?" he asked Billings.

"Yeah, it is," he shouted over the piercing noise. "But we don't have any drills scheduled for right now, especially since there's surgery going on downstairs."

Billings took a step back and began to talk into the radio he'd pulled from his hip.

Kenneth reached out for Willa and took her hand.

Her eyes were wide.

He gave her hand what he hoped was a reassuring squeeze.

Billings stepped closer. "There's someone attacking staff downstairs outside room 203!"

Kenneth's heartbeat galloped to attention.

Room 203 was where Leonard Bartow was supposed to be. It was only on the recommendation of Detective Lovett that Leonard had been moved to another room after the second attack on Willa. "It might not do us any good to be the only ones who know where he really is, but it might do whoever is helping him or involved some bad to not know where he really is," he'd reasoned.

Maybe Foster had been right.

"I have to go," Billings yelled over the alarm. He started to turn but Kenneth grabbed his uniformed arm in an invasive move and kept him steady. He pointed at the door and at Willa.

"You guard them. I'll go downstairs!"

Kenneth didn't wait for an audible confirmation. He did wait for Willa's.

"Go," she insisted.

So, he did.

Gun out and ready for anything.

WILLA DIDN'T LIKE it but she was ushered into the room Billings had been guarding and right into the sights of Leonard Bartow. True to the guard's words, the big man was attached to the hospital bed by a set of handcuffs.

When their eyes met, it was instant recognition.

Willa made sure not to reach up and touch the skin of her neck that was still slightly bruised from the brute's hands. The foundation her sister had given her was the only reason no one had so far commented on it.

"What's that damn noise for?" Leonard yelled at Billings.

He didn't answer him.

"I'm going to be right outside the door," he said to Willa instead. "No one will be coming in but me or your detective."

Willa cast Leonard an uncertain look.

Billings caught it. "He's cuffed and I'm the only one with a key. You'll be fine."

Billings's concern for her was nothing compared to Kenneth's. He was out the door, letting it shut behind him, in a second flat.

Then again, guarding Leonard and her had been his most recent directive.

"What's going on?" Her former attacker's voice was filled with a mixture of anxiety and anger. The same thing she was feeling just looking at him.

"That's the fire alarm," she responded, pointing up. The noise wasn't as deafening in the room but they still had to raise their voices.

"If there's a fire then why are we still in here?" His anxiety notched up to an easily discernible panic as he pulled on the handcuffs. They stayed right where they were on the bed rail.

"It's an alarm, I don't know if there's an actual fire," she snapped. Her own rising panic wasn't as easy to control.

Was it a coincidence that the moment they were about to talk to Leonard, the fire alarm went off? That some man was fighting people downstairs outside the room the sheriff's department had moved him from?

No.

There was absolutely no way in hell.

Willa worried for Kenneth with such acuteness that she physically grabbed at her chest as she looked back at the closed door.

"You were with Detective Gray, weren't you?"

The question caught Willa wholly off guard. So

much so, she told the truth and nodded. "Yes, he was about to walk in when the alarm went off. He had to go downstairs to check it out."

The man might have looked like an ogre but it almost seemed like he was doing some figures in his head, working something out.

To her shock, he had.

"He wouldn't have left you here to go downstairs if there was a fire. He would have taken you with him." Leonard's frown deepened.

The fire alarm cut off.

The silence behind his words was eerie as he continued. "He's coming for me because I'm a loose end."

Willa wasn't about to dismiss the thought. She took a tentative step toward him.

"Who is he? Who are you—?"

A sound that was becoming all too familiar to Willa made her scream.

It was a gunshot and it had been out in the hallway.

Willa didn't have time to react further before two more shots sounded.

She was clutching at her shirt, terror thronging through her body, when Leonard's voice managed to penetrate her fear.

"Get in the bathroom, Miss Tate."

It was a simple, straightforward statement said in a calm, even tone.

Willa looked Leonard's way because, for that moment, he was the only sturdy thing in the room.

"Don't make a sound," he added.

Someone yelled out in the hallway. Another gunshot sounded.

It was enough to make her move.

Willa hurried into the attached bathroom. She shut the door and turned out the light. Not even a second later, the door to the other room banged open.

She placed her hands over her mouth, hoping to hear Billings or, even better, Kenneth.

Instead the only voice she heard belonged to a stranger.

He was loud and quick.

"Sorry."

It took everything Willa had not to scream as one last gunshot went off.

Chapter Sixteen

The bathroom was dark but the light from the room poured inside and surrounded the woman.

Kenneth could have cried in relief.

"Willa?" He dropped his gun to his side and flipped on the light. Her wide, worried eyes took him in as his did the same to her.

She didn't appear to be hurt.

"There was a man…" she started. "I heard him say sorry and—" She placed a hand over her mouth. "Oh God, he shot Billings and Leonard, didn't he? They're dead, aren't they?"

One day he wished the only news he would give Willa was good. He couldn't control that now.

"Yes. They are."

Willa's eyes welled with tears. Kenneth could hear security and responding deputies running through the halls. It had been over ten minutes since the fire in the stairwell had been set, the man downstairs had attacked a nurse and a patient, and the barrage of bullets could be heard exploding overhead. When Kenneth realized his error, his grave mistake of leaving Willa's side despite promising not to, it had felt like his feet hadn't even had time to touch the ground with how fast he ran up the stairs that weren't blocked.

His stomach had fallen to his feet when he'd seen Billings on the ground outside the open door.

Then Leonard, motionless in his bed.

Kenneth didn't know what he would have done had he opened the bathroom door and Willa not been there.

"Are you hurt?" he asked, reaching out to take her hand.

Willa shook her head. Those tears began to spill over her cheeks.

"No but I… I'd very much like to leave here," she stammered out. "If…if we can."

Kenneth hated to keep the bad news coming.

"We can, but not yet. The hospital is on lockdown until the man who did this is found. So I'm going to need you to stay in here for a little bit longer. Okay?"

Willa shook her head but repeated his last word.

"Oh…okay."

Kenneth dropped her hand and positioned himself in the open doorway of the bathroom. Out of his periphery he saw Willa move against the wall behind the door, blocking any and all sight into Leonard's room. Thankfully, from their angle, the blood from both Leonard and Billings couldn't be seen.

The hospital was in lockdown but it started to fill up with law enforcement. Even reserve deputies came out and each floor was swept from top to bottom for the mystery man. Detective Lovett had been one of the first to show and had called Kenneth after reviewing the security footage.

"He knew where to walk to avoid being seen head-on by the cameras," Lovett had said, his words heated. "I can't see his face for anything, just like I can't see how he got in or if he got out."

After that call, Kenneth had made several others. All while keeping his spot in the doorway and his hand on his gun.

He didn't move an inch when the sheriff or his other colleagues arrived to work the scene. By the time the county coroner and friend to the department, Dr. Amanda Alvarez, appeared, the search within the hospital was done.

"It would be better to take her out now and have her close her eyes than wait," she told Kenneth in a low voice. "Things will get messier before they get cleaner."

"Thank you," he replied, taking the thoughtfulness for Willa to heart.

He also took the advice.

"We're going to leave, but I need you to close your eyes, Willa."

The woman had no objections. In fact, she didn't say a word as Kenneth decided picking her up and carrying her past Leonard and over Billings's body would be the best way to keep her from having to deal with haunting images.

"We're in the elevator now, so I'm going to put you down, okay?"

Willa nodded but didn't open her eyes until her feet

were against the floor. Kenneth pushed the button for the lobby. Willa stayed against him, silent.

"Are we going home?" Her voice was so small, so soft.

Kenneth found himself nodding.

"Yes. I've already cleared it with the sheriff. We can go."

The car ride was, he suspected, much like the one the night before. This time, however, their situations were reversed. Willa kept quiet while Kenneth worried mindlessly for her until he was able to take her into his house and set her down on the couch.

There her silence broke into a flood of tears.

"He…he told me to hide in the bathroom after the first shot."

Kenneth pulled her against him, cradling her much like she had him after LeAnne's death.

"Who? Leonard?"

She nodded, her hair brushing up against the bottom of his chin.

"He…he told me not to make a sound. I don't understand. Why did…why did he do that?"

Kenneth stroked the back of her hair and held her tight.

He admitted he didn't know.

She continued to cry until her sobs slowed into deep breaths. Then into a quiet that managed to fill up the room.

Every tear, every gasp, and every breath, Kenneth felt in his bones.

"I want you to stay here tonight," he said with nothing but honesty.

It wasn't a question but Willa still gave him an answer.

"Okay."

After that their world sped up a little. Willa excused herself to the bathroom and then called her sister while Kenneth made several calls of his own. The witnesses who had seen the fight told their descriptions of the gunman but it didn't sound like anyone they recognized. It was only luck that Kenneth saw two bandages on the man's right arm in the security footage from where his sleeve had slipped down. That was enough to make them suspect that he was, in fact, the man in the hockey mask who had killed LeAnne, his bandages hiding cuts he'd gotten from his and Kenneth's tussle. There was an all-points-bulletin out on him and a sketch artist from the next county was coming over to work with them to see if they couldn't put his face out there since he'd avoided the hospital's security cameras.

Everything else on the technical side of what had happened was being handled by the sheriff. He'd been the one to suggest taking Willa somewhere else and keeping an eye on her.

Regardless, even if he hadn't, that's exactly what Kenneth would have done.

Because, as much as he hated to admit it, it felt like two things were happening at once and neither of them was good.

Someone was cleaning up loose ends and someone considered Willa part of that mess.

THAT NIGHT CAME to find Willa in better spirits.

Though *better* was starting to become a relative term.

She wasn't better compared to her life before she'd found the box, but she was a lot better than she had been before two people near her had been shot dead while she'd hid in the bathroom.

The worst part about finding the box was the constant death it seemed to bring with it.

The best part about finding the box was the man who woke her from her nap to offer her a peanut butter and jelly sandwich for dinner.

"I almost let you keep sleeping but realized I couldn't remember if you'd eaten anything for lunch," he said. "Also, not trying to push, but your sister has already called me twice. I think she wants to talk to you and not hear from me that you're okay."

Willa smiled, not an ounce embarrassed.

"Good of you to wake me. Though I barely convinced her to go stay at Kimball's parents' place. I'm not sure she'll believe I'm okay."

Kenneth slid her the phone and excused himself to give her some privacy. She ate her sandwich and spoke to Martha until it was gone.

"You should be with me," Martha insisted one last time before the call ended.

Not if I'm a target, Willa thought, and not for the first time. She skirted repeating that and took a more judicious route.

"This is only temporary, Martha. I'm good here, and you know that."

Martha didn't respond with anything cheerful but did

let Willa off of the phone without any more pushback.
Then it was time to finally return the several texts from
Ebony, though Willa did so with a call. Guilt at keeping
what was happening from her faded away as she gave
the Cliff's Notes version of everything that had gone
on since she'd found the box.

Ebony had, understandably, freaked out.

Then she'd reverted to nothing but concern. She'd
asked Willa what she'd needed and accepted her answer
of time alone to process.

Or, at least, time alone with the only person who she
felt safe being with.

Willa ended the call with promises of checking in
later and took her plate to the kitchen. Kenneth was finishing off his sandwich over the sink. He grinned and
took the dish from her.

"I hope you don't mind my lack of chef's excellence,"
he said. "As you probably saw this morning, I need to
go grocery shopping something fierce."

Willa situated herself leaning against the counter so
she was facing him. He made quick work of cleaning
the plate, despite the dishwasher being close by.

"You won't find me complaining," she assured him,
weirdly warmed by his show of domestic gumption. "I
was hungry and that *was* a great sandwich."

Kenneth chuckled. He dried off his hands.

The conversation hit a small lull.

Delilah, dropped off by Kimball along with a bag of
Willa's things packed by Martha right after lunch, de-
cided to break it with some pointed licks to her hand.
It made Willa laugh.

"You know, for a moment, I think Kimball was thinking about asking if Delilah could stay with them a bit longer." Willa scratched behind Delilah's ear. Something she seemed to be very fond of. "I wouldn't be surprised if, when this is all over, he talks Martha into getting their own puppy."

"Can you blame him? Look at this stunner."

Kenneth surprised her by heading to the living room and dropping down into a crouch. Delilah became hyper at the movement and followed, as did Willa. Delilah lapped at his face while he rubbed down her sides, exciting her even more. She gave a few barks and then was pure speed as she ran out of the room in a wild gallop. It made the humans in the house laugh.

"And that's what you call the zoomies," Kenneth explained. "She's about to treat this place like an Indy 500 track, slow down long enough to need to go outside, and then she'll pass out shortly after."

"Ah, such a simple life sounds fantastic right about now."

True to his word, Delilah zoomed around the house. She managed to get both of them to chase her, extending the fun until, sure enough, she ran to the back door and barked.

"Coming through," Kenneth called, running from his spot behind the couch where he'd been playing hide-and-seek with her. Willa laughed from her spot behind a chair opposite. She went to the back door and watched as the fully grown man resembled a carefree kid, running around in the backyard. It was only after Delilah did her business that he slowed.

And it was only when he led the dog inside the house that the carefree kid turned back into an adult.

The one with bills and fears and pain.

But maybe Willa was projecting her mood again.

Because, for all of the smiles and laughter she'd taken part in, there was a growing weight that couldn't be ignored.

It must have showed on her face.

When Delilah went to lap up some water from the kitchen, Willa admitted that she was still tired. And that there was a good chance some of that was from a collection of bad days and not just what had happened at the hospital.

"It just feels like we've been trying to walk up a hill while it storms," she said. "Every step we take up, we slide back two."

Kenneth sighed. It was an impressive sight from how close she was standing next to him. He was in an undershirt since being home and it was tight enough that the movement showed a hint of lean, muscled chest. Though she'd already seen his upper body when she'd made him change at the hospital the day before, there was something different about seeing even a tease of it now.

Or maybe she was just getting caught up in more and more details about the man.

His shirt, his cleaning habits, how his eyes crinkled at the sides when he laughed while playing with his dog. How he'd handed her a napkin with her plated sandwich.

How he'd let her into his home to protect her.

How he was looking at her now, making her feel like she was the only person in the world.

Those eyes of his, filled with depth and a storm-clouded sky, empathized with her.

"Believe it or not, I know how that feels."

He motioned her to follow him and was soon giving her a rundown on his bathroom and the shower, if she wanted to take a spin, as he called it.

"All my bath soap and shampoo smells like cologne, but it'll at least get the job done cleaning-wise if Martha didn't pack yours," he said, showing her the various bottles lining the shelf in the shower. "There're also clean towels in that closet and, if you're feeling fancy, a robe I may or may not have accidentally stolen from a hotel in Kipsy, Alabama, when I went to visit a friend last year. Don't worry, it's clean, too."

"I have to say, Mr. Gray, you're very accommodating," she said.

The man smirked, more playful than usual. "Something all men love to hear from a beautiful woman."

That made Willa's cheeks burn up in an instant. Luckily, Kenneth had excused himself to give her some privacy. But that didn't stop her from thinking about the comment as she showered and readied for bed.

When she was finished and dressed in her flannel pajama set that looked like it belonged in a family Christmas movie, Willa hoped the blush that was lying low beneath the surface would stay there.

No such luck when she saw that Kenneth had changed, too.

Instead of jeans, he was wearing a pair of nearly matching flannel sleep pants.

"Well, great minds, I guess?" she said, pointing to the obvious.

Kenneth chuckled. "I have to say I think you wear them better."

That blush lifted itself to her face again. She had no choice but to fight through it, especially when she saw a bandage peeking out of his shirtsleeve.

It was like cold water to her face.

Another two steps back on the hill.

Kenneth didn't notice at first. He was moving around the bed, adding a new blanket.

"I'm going to give you the bed, and don't try to talk me out of it because that's a fight you'll lose. I'll take the couch downstairs," he said, unaware that the mere mention of him being somewhere else made Willa's anxiety rise. "As for Delilah, you're going to have to keep the door shut to keep her out. She's gotten used to sleeping on the bed because *someone* has let her do it almost every night of her life."

He cracked a grin and finally faced her with full attention.

"What's wrong?" He was all serious in a second flat.

Willa averted her gaze. Then thought, *Who cares?*

They'd already been through a lot together as it was. She looked him in the eye.

What would this hurt?

"Could you stay with me? At least until I fall asleep?"

It sounded like a simple request—and maybe it really was simple—but Willa felt her heartbeat speed up as the questions came out.

Never mind when Kenneth didn't even blink before he answered.

"I won't say no to that."

Chapter Seventeen

Willa slipped beneath the cool sheets, taking extreme care not to touch Kenneth as she did so. It wasn't for lack of want—hadn't she struggled with the fact that she *knew* she wanted the detective for the last week?—but out of respect.

And…well, fear.

Not the sickening kind that had gone through her several times recently.

No.

This fear had everything to do with her feelings. Her desires.

The fact that she didn't know if they were reciprocated by the detective.

Or, to be truthful, deserved.

That thought rattled her more than she'd meant it to and, no sooner had the man been laid out on his side of the bed, than Willa finally give voice to a thought that had been growing unchecked within her.

"It's my fault," she said. "It's all my fault."

Kenneth was on his back but readjusted to look at her, his hands behind his head and elbows against the pillow. If she had thought he was a big man when standing, he somehow seemed to command a bigger presence in the bed. Willa felt tiny in comparison.

"Because you found the box and didn't let it go."

Willa nodded because he was exactly right.

"Three people have died and, why? Because I wanted to solve a mystery? And what if there's nothing really there to begin with? What if it was just a box of random things like you first said?" Willa rolled onto her back and stared up at the ceiling. The only light in the room was on the nightstand next to Kenneth. It was small and cast shadows against the popcorn ceiling. "What if everything that's happened could have been avoided had I just kept my mouth shut and my curiosity at bay?"

Willa thought of LeAnne, Billings, and even Leonard.

They would all be alive had she done things differently.

The sound of fabric moving against skin preceded Kenneth's hand sliding beneath the covers to find hers.

The contact startled her but she didn't move away.

Instead, she listened to the warm rumble of his voice.

"I've never told you about the day Ally died, have I?"

That question was more unexpected than the impromptu hand-hold. Willa shook her head. He must have heard the movement because he continued without a verbal answer.

"Most know the gist of how she was found, in Becker's field with two bullets in her, but no one knows why she was there in the first place." He shifted a little but kept Willa's hand. His voice stayed even and warm despite the topic. "See, Ally was one of those crazy people who loved to run. I'd say it's all just exercise and she'd fuss at me and say running wasn't just a way to try to stay in shape, it was a lifestyle. A way to get and keep control of your life while also giving you freedom."

He laughed. It sounded old and worn.

A laugh recalled from a memory he'd no doubt had with his wife.

"But for me? Well, it was just a fast way to make you sweaty and hungry." Willa felt through the mattress's rising and falling that he'd taken a deep breath. When he'd let the breath out, the warmth in his voice had gone with it. "The last time I saw her alive, she wanted to break in her new running shoes and go on a trail at the park to shake things up. She asked me to go with her. I didn't."

There was unmistakable pain in his voice.

Willa wished she could make it better. She knew she couldn't. At least, not entirely.

"No one knows where she was actually killed, just knew that she wasn't shot there in Becker's," he continued. "And to this day, I have no idea what would have happened had I gone with her instead of staying home. So, I blamed myself then for her death just as I still blame myself now sometimes for it, too."

"But you didn't do anything wrong," Willa piped in. "You couldn't have known what would happen."

As she said the words, Willa realized why Kenneth was telling her about Ally now instead of all the times they'd been together in the last week.

He gave her hand a squeeze of pressure.

"Unless you came up with the plan, carried it out, and

pulled the trigger, it isn't your fault." He sighed again. It sounded lighter somehow. "But I know it's a hard truth to accept. What-if scenarios put bumps in the road to acceptance."

Willa started at that.

"Well, if that isn't a poetic way to put it, Mr. Gray. I'm impressed."

The mattress moved as his laugh rumbled through it.

"You have my mom to thank for that," he said when he was done. "She more or less said that same thing about a hundred times after I left the department the first time. I guess it stuck."

"You're just taking the long way 'round to healing if you keep tormenting yourself with what could have been and how things would have turned out had you chosen differently. It's a good sentiment."

Kenneth laughed again and this time he rolled over onto his side, sliding one arm beneath the pillow and letting her hand go with the other. Willa mimicked the move. She was on her side, facing him, hands in a prayer stance between her cheek on the pillowcase. Suddenly it felt like two friends at a sleepover, shooting the breeze about life, love, and also trivial things.

Never mind that they were in their thirties, had both survived attacks meant to kill in the last few days, and were a single man and a single woman.

"You know, I was born in Kelby Creek and grew up here, and I've heard a lot of Southernisms, but 'long way 'round' is new even to me. When we met, it was the first time I'd heard it."

Willa snorted.

"I have a theory on that," she said. "See, there are tiers of being Southern and only us top-tier families use phrases like that. 'Like a hair in a biscuit,' 'madder than a wet hen,' 'full as a tick,' 'worn slap out,' and so on. 'Long way 'round' is just something I grew up hearing from my family. Though it can be a pain in the backside to use when you're trying to give someone directions on where not to go, especially since the long way 'round isn't just a measurement of distance."

"It isn't?"

She shook her head. Willa had washed her hair but had quickly braided it to her scalp. It would be a mess in the morning when she unleashed it, but she was trying to save the man's pillow from being soaked through. She'd gone through his bathroom cabinets and there wasn't a hair dryer to be found. There was nothing, in fact, aimed for use by a woman. It had split her emotions down the middle.

On the one hand, she imagined Kenneth cleaning out Ally's things after her death, maybe slowly or maybe through the years. On the other hand, she was pleased to see that no other woman seemed to have been entertained by the man in recent years. Or, if they had been, they'd brought their toiletries in and then taken them out.

Willa's braids smelled like spice and something woodsy as she shifted her head to look up at him a little more easily. It wasn't an unpleasant thing.

"Sometimes it just means you took the challenging way. The road less traveled."

"I suppose that makes sense. Though my favorite

Southernism hands down will always be 'bless your heart.'" He grinned. "I've never heard nastier fighting words than those."

"Ugh. I *hate* that phrase," Willa said, honest as a nun in church. "Your contractor's—Landon Mitchell— mother used to say it to me all the time. She disapproved of my job, my hair, and my disinterest in learning to knit. I mean…don't get me wrong, I don't judge those who do knit, but after she told me I needed to do it to be a good mom, I made a promise to myself to never touch a knitting needle out of pure pettiness." She shook her head. "That woman blessed my heart so many times it'll probably get to heaven before the rest of me ever follows."

That really got Kenneth going. He was laughing so much that it turned her growing grumpiness at the memories into following his contagious laughter with her own. It was nice to hear the man happy. It was nice to be the reason why he was smiling, too.

"I never would have guessed someone could dislike you at all," Kenneth said after he'd composed himself. "You remind me of sunshine, and who dislikes sunshine?"

Willa didn't know how he'd meant the compliment to land but it was a powerful hit. She was glad he couldn't see her cheeks that were, no doubt, flaming to life.

"People have called me bubbly and bouncy, but I'm not sure anyone has ever said I was like sunshine."

He hesitated. The first time he'd done so all night.

"Not even Landon?"

Willa shook her head again. She wondered if he

could read the change in emotion moving through her chest.

"No."

It was a simple response. A true one.

And Kenneth responded with only three simple words before the house around them became quiet.

"Bless his heart."

ON SATURDAY MORNING answers started to come in.

Much like the rain.

Willa emerged from his room around eight, dressed and with her hair still in braids. She held up her phone to show a social media post from their local news station.

"The weatherman promised no more rain for a week after today."

Kenneth didn't rightly believe him.

By the time noon rolled around, he was sure it had been raining for years.

An annoyance that normally wouldn't have affected him, not being able to go outside felt limiting. Plus, the man who'd entered the hospital hadn't been found. Neither by the all-points-bulletin nor from their working sketch thanks to witnesses at the hospital. Whoever he was, he wasn't in the department's system and he hadn't made a scene outside the hospital. That only made the rain more frustrating.

It limited their search and it improved his chances of staying hidden.

Willa brought Delilah in from a quick bathroom break in the yard, shucking rain off the umbrella, and in an increasingly foul mood. Earlier that morning she had been doing her own investigation into the developer who had bought the lot where the box had been buried and was still waiting for a call-back from someone.

"I know I didn't tell them about the urgency of the matter but, still, it's only polite that when you say you're going to call back in a few minutes you actually call back within a few minutes. Not make the person you promised wait."

She grabbed for the towel Kenneth had put next to the side door to the yard and absently began to pat dry Delilah, who sat still, used to the process.

"I swear, Dee, you've got better manners than most humans," Willa muttered.

Kenneth had overtaken his dining room table despite having an office to utilize. He blamed the paperwork that was starting to pile up across its surface but, the truth was, the night before had changed something between him and Willa.

At least, in his mind.

Kenneth had already believed Willa to be a beautiful woman, but the sight of her sleeping in his bed, wet braids dampening his pillow, hands folded against her cheek, face slack and at peace, had utterly bewitched him.

She was a light in the darkness.

Not just sunshine. She was the moon in the night sky, too.

It was another poetic statement—though, this one he kept inside his head—that he hadn't known he believed.

But he did.

That's why he decided to work at the dining room

table. It gave them both room to work together. Even if it was in silence, it was a companionable one.

The kind he enjoyed just as much as watching her do the simplest of things like wiping the rain off Delilah or asking him if he wanted anything while she was up.

Kenneth knew that part of that might be the fact that he had been lonely over the last few years, shying away from true connection, but the other part?

That was all Willa.

The woman let Delilah run wild while she tucked back into the kitchen. She offered him a fresh cup of coffee, which he said he'd gladly accept.

It was still brewing when his phone starting ringing.

The Caller ID read Foster Lovett.

Kenneth answered on the second ring. "Gray here."

There was a rustling on Lovett's side of the phone. He asked Kenneth to give him a second.

Willa came in with an empty coffee mug, curious. She watched him as Lovett found a better position to talk.

"Sorry, this rain is a kink in the kitchen sink, I tell you." He didn't wait for a response. "Gray, we found a few things that we don't have context for yet but…well, it's a heck of a few things."

Kenneth got that feeling in his gut. That *everything is about to change* feeling.

But, like life, there was no other way through it than to go through it, so he said, "Okay, hit me."

Lovett took a breath. The noise behind him had quieted considerably. He must be inside now.

"We ran down who the ring belonged to, or did years ago."

"Who?" Kenneth grabbed his pen.

"A Joshua Kepler from out of town bought it eight years ago, and the only reason why the owner of the jeweler's remembered his name and the ring is that Joshua used to have a different last name when he lived in Kelby Creek. Linderman."

"Linderman?"

Willa's eyes widened as Kenneth wrote down the name.

"Josiah Linderman's son."

Kenneth couldn't believe it. He said as much but then that feeling came back when Lovett said that wasn't all. Not by a mile.

"You're at home now, right?" Lovett asked before explaining. "Willa is still there with you, too?"

"I am," Kenneth said slowly. "She is."

Willa mouthed "what," but Kenneth's attention had been pooling around the phone call until there was nothing but Lovett's voice.

He sounded reluctant and sorry all at the same time.

"The bullet casing inside the box… Well, after looking into old unsolved cases, we actually found the bullet it matched."

Kenneth knew then. He wrote down the name but waited for the detective to finish before dropping his pen.

"Gray, the casing matched one of the bullets that killed your wife."

Chapter Eighteen

Willa was in the kitchen while the sheriff and a deputy she didn't recognize spoke with Kenneth in his home office. It wasn't at his behest that they get more privacy, but Willa could tell that the news had knocked Kenneth off whatever balance they'd become comfortable with since they'd met.

Willa wasn't surprised.

Though she wished she knew the full extent of what was going on, and not just what Kenneth, as if in a daze, had repeated to her after the phone call had ended.

It was while she was feeling sad for Kenneth and trying to foresee what the news of the potentially connected cases would do to their investigation that the phone call she'd been waiting for came in.

A man named Ronaldo said hello and all the nice things you said to a stranger on the phone before asking what he could do for her.

"I'm the office manager with Clanton Construction here in Kelby Creek. I was updating some files and realized the file on the town houses on lot 427 in town had been misplaced. I was hoping to fix that, if I could, by next week so my boss doesn't think I'm lousy with a computer."

Willa hurried to grab the notebook that Kenneth had let her borrow and searched out a pen. "I've managed to find most of the information, like your company, Red Tree Development, is the one that purchased the lot and hired us to do the work. But there's a spot here for the person who was in charge of accepting our bid. Mrs. Reynolds from your office said that that information was with you, which is why I left the message with her to pass on."

Willa had learned at an early age that if you talked long enough, made the words sweet enough, and gave the person you were talking to the chance to be a hero, most people were mighty inclined to help.

Ronaldo was definitely one of those people.

"Ah, I certainly can get that information for you, Miss Tate," he exclaimed. "You're in luck because I often work from home and all of my information is here. Give me a second to get my computer booted up."

They talked non-talk for a little bit—professional chitchat, as she liked to call it—until he'd brought up the Clanton Construction account.

"Ah, Lot 427. The town houses…" he said. "Let's see… Well, won't you know it. There are three people listed here with Red Tree who helped facilitate the bid and buy. I'm afraid I don't have more details other than their names, but their contact information would be on the company web site."

"Oh, that's okay. I just need to put down the names. If we need more, I can reach out later."

Ronaldo gave her all three names and wished her luck with her computer skills, something that made Willa blush considering she'd lied.

And then she was left staring at three names she didn't recognize.

Maria Clements, Nadja Loren, and Terry Page.

Willa was about to Google them when the men came out of Kenneth's office.

Not a one of them looked happy.

Willa put her notebook back on the dining table and smiled at the group. The sheriff took his tried-and-true cowboy hat off, gave her a nod, and said he had to get going. The deputy followed.

Kenneth shut the door behind them.

He locked it.

Willa took a tentative step forward. She didn't know what to say, let alone ask.

Thankfully, Kenneth had become more forthright with her. Instead of leading her to the table or the office, he took a heavy seat on the couch. Willa was much more delicate as she perched on the cushion next to him, angling her body to face him.

"They were looking through cold cases with the same kind of caliber bullet that matched the casing found in the box," he started, no segue. "They found only two unsolved in the last thirty years with the same kind—Ally's and an older man who'd been killed in a robbery gone wrong. Ally's was the only case where a bullet and one casing were missing. The one in the box was a perfect match with the one that was…was in her."

Willa took his hand. At this point, it was something

they'd both done several times. It didn't faze either of them.

"So what does that mean?" she asked, hoping some of her warmth would seep through her skin and right into his heart. She hated how tense he'd become since the call.

Kenneth let out a long breath.

"It means that, somehow, Josiah Linderman and Ally are connected. Whether it's by a killer or something else, I don't know."

Willa again couldn't believe that one box could cause such confusion and devastation.

She also couldn't believe what he repeated from Detective Lovett to her next. Not only had Joshua Linderman come back to town, the engagement ring he'd bought had been found in the box too.

It was a lot to process.

"What about Joshua Linderman? Or is it Joshua Kepler? Maybe he can tell us something?"

"That's what Detective Lovett is deep-diving on now. Our best guess for his name change is that, after he went into the foster care system, he was adopted by a family and changed his last name to theirs. Foster is trying to find Joshua through his new name but so far he can't locate him."

"What about their uncle? I could reach out to him again. Maybe he knows more about the children than he let on about the first time around. Why else would Joshua be back in town?"

Kenneth nodded. It was like he'd aged ten years within half an hour. "That would be nice."

Had this been at their first meeting, Willa would have gone about her task without another word. But now she could tell there was something that Kenneth was holding back.

She moved her hand from his and brought it up to his cheek. "What else?"

A smile passed over his lips. It was brief.

"Josiah's most prized picture, Joshua's engagement ring, and the bullet that helped kill my wife… I'm now almost afraid to know how the bloody cloth that used to be in there connects. And why it was the only item stolen from the box."

"Do you still think the man in the hockey mask is the one who stole it from my apartment before Leonard showed up?"

It was a theory they'd kicked around earlier that morning. Why else would the man at the hospital walk in and kill Leonard the way that he had?

Kenneth nodded.

"I think Leonard was about to tell me who his partner was, or his employer, if he was a hired hand, and I think that's why he was taken out. He's the only one who could have given us real answers. Not just conjecture and theories—which, by the way, I'm not a fan of."

Willa let her hand slide down to his chin. "We'll get to the bottom of all this."

She didn't need to do it, but she did.

Willa used her hand to tilt his chin down enough so she could place a chaste kiss on his lips.

When she pulled back, it took him a bit longer than usual to look up from her lips to her eyes.

"That's the fourth kiss," he noted. His voice unreadable. "What was it for?"

Willa smiled.

"Faith."

Kenneth tried to return the smile but it didn't last. The three names she'd found slipped right out of her mind as the need to talk to Josiah's brother-in-law took over. Surely, he had answers.

At some point someone had to.

JOSIAH LINDERMAN'S FORMER brother-in-law was less talkative about Josiah and Mae's children than he had been about his sister. Mostly because he'd felt guilty, as he said in his own words, that he wasn't able to take the children and that's how they'd wound up in foster care.

"I already told you I didn't take them in. I was having my own problems and…well, I couldn't raise no kids. The last time I even saw 'em young was right after Josiah went missin'. Didn't seem to be anything I could say to be helpful and I knew if they saw me again, it would make it hard for everyone."

Willa had been delicate about how she handled the rest of the conversation—she wasn't blaming him or anyone for the choices made in the wake of tragedy.

"You said the last time you saw them was when they were young. So does that mean you haven't seen them as adults?"

Turns out, he had. Something he'd kept from both her and Kenneth the times they'd called before.

"I'd heard Joshua had come back in to pay some respects to his mama's grave on the anniversary of her death. I went out to find him there." Willa could hear the pride in his next statement. "He looked good. Tall and healthy, you know. Smart, too. Said he'd found a family who liked him to read a lot, and so he'd learned a thing or two. He even said he'd gotten him a woman who liked books and all of that, too. Said he was thinking about marrying her but had to do some things first."

He didn't know what those things were and, when Willa asked if Joshua spoke of his sister, Mariam, he was openly upset by his own answer.

"Joshua said him and Mariam got split up in care when they both were still real young. She got adopted a year before him and they'd kept up with letters for a while but then lost each other." He cussed. "We can only hope she got as lucky as he did."

There wasn't anything else to ask once he admitted that was the last time he'd seen Joshua, and the last of what he knew about him.

Willa bid the man a thank-you and a goodbye, feeling a heaviness in her heart as she did so.

A family that had started out steeped in what people called true love between Josiah and Mae had turned into mystery and loss.

Willa wished she could snap her fingers and make it all go away. Bring back Mae, keep Josiah from walking to the store that day, and watch Joshua and Mariam be raised by two caring parents.

But she couldn't and she went to the bathroom to become weepy about it for a few minutes.

By the time she was done, Kenneth was off the phone and ready to listen to what she'd learned. He conferenced Foster in on the call and both men were quiet as she recalled the conversation.

"Finding kids in care, who aged out of care, and who were adopted, is a hard get in Alabama, so finding Mariam might be a lot harder than we hope," Foster commented when she was done. "Especially since Joshua is our only lead and he apparently lost touch with her."

"What about Joshua?" Kenneth asked. "Any luck with Cadence Jewelers' owner and tracking down any information on him?"

"The owner's still looking through his boxes of records but thinks we can get an address off of the receipt when he finds it. I'll keep you updated. On everything. Thanks for the help, Willa. And, Gray? Can you switch off speakerphone?"

Willa used the need for privacy to take Delilah out into the backyard. The rain had downgraded to a drizzle but was in a way refreshing. She tried to forget for a moment how quickly life could change for the good or the bad and turned her face up to the sky.

After a minute or so, she felt better.

She took Delilah back inside, patted the pup off, and found Kenneth in the kitchen.

He was staring out the window.

"I know this question is becoming moot, but is everything okay?" she asked.

"I've had better days, I suppose." Kenneth snorted. "That is one reason the sheriff has decided that I need to take the rest of the afternoon off. 'Take it easy while you can.'"

"You don't strike me as a man who appreciates that suggestion."

Willa moved to lean against the counter, facing him again. The casual stance was becoming a habit the longer she was in the house.

"I'm not good at sitting still. Usually when I'm alone with my thoughts, I end up being as far from relaxed as possible."

Willa shrugged, silently conceding that a lot of people rarely got peace of mind when alone with their thoughts.

"*But* you're not alone now," she said, smiling wide and true. "I'm here."

She was about to list off reasons why the sheriff's advice wasn't bad—being run ragged never helped anyone, half the department including the lead detective was working on every angle of their investigation, and they themselves were really just waiting for callbacks—but then Kenneth did something peculiar.

He just stopped and stared down at her.

Willa felt her cheeks heating up. Her eyebrow rose in question.

She didn't get a chance to ask a thing.

Kenneth went from standing tall to swooping low. His lips pressed against Willa's moments before his arms encircled her.

In that moment, the world went out the window as far as she was concerned.

It was made up of just two people, kissing in the kitchen.

Kenneth did not seem to want to keep that status for long, however.

One fluid motion was all it took for the detective to take her from standing to up in his arms and then on top of the counter itself. A glass clinked against the top as her backside must have pushed it aside. It was loud enough to make Kenneth pause.

He broke their kiss to inspect the clatter.

"Are you okay?" he asked, voice filled with gravel that felt like it was rubbing against all the right places on her. "Willa?"

That pulled her attention from her hammering heartbeat but didn't give him the answer he wanted.

"What was that kiss for?" she found herself asking.

He might have thought it a play on their already-established small kiss inside joke. But, for Willa, it was exactly the question she wanted answered.

The absolute lack of smile but very present loosening of control was a good sign.

"That was because I want you." Slower than the last time, tentative almost, Kenneth pressed his lips back to hers. It was tender but deep. Willa had to force her eyes open when he pulled back. "That was to show you the first wasn't a fluke. And—" He came back for another kiss.

It was torture. Willa loved it, though not so much when he stepped back again.

"—that was to hopefully give you a taste of the rest of my intentions."

Willa sounded more breathless than she felt.

She did manage a smile, though.

"How about now we just assume that anything that

happens between us is because we both, really, really want it? No need to stop and talk about it."

Kenneth's eyes became hooded. Then his gaze went to her lips.

"Sounds like a plan to me."

Chapter Nineteen

The rain had stopped sometime in the middle of the night.

Kenneth only noted the lack of sound because in its place was something better. At least, to him.

Willa Tate didn't snore, but she made this small murmur on occasion as she slept. It wasn't something he'd witnessed the night before when he'd stayed until she'd fallen asleep but, after remaining in the bed with her, a long while after she'd fallen asleep, he'd been able to listen to the soft murmur until he'd also drifted off. Before that, he'd watched her sleep, stroked her hair when her cheek was against his collarbone, and then marveled at how warm she was when he pulled her flush against him, arm over her hip protectively.

That's how he'd woken up the first time early Sunday morning.

Willa under his arm and back to his chest.

He'd felt her breathing in and out and was happier for it.

Happier than he'd been in a long, long while.

So much so, he dozed off until an hour or so later.

Willa wasn't in his arms any longer, but she was still in his bed. He blinked a few times before realizing she was awake and staring at the ceiling. Her brows were knitted together in a way that made him instantly alert.

"What is it?"

Willa jumped a little. He reached out and found her hand beneath the covers. He realized then that they were both still naked but didn't comment on it just yet. Not when she looked so concerned about something.

"Sorry," he added. "I didn't mean to startle you."

Willa's cheeks flushed but she gave him a small, dismissive wave with her free hand.

"Oh, don't worry. I probably am the one who woke you with my moving around. Sorry."

Now she really had his attention. her voice sounded off.

Kenneth rolled onto his side and propped himself up to look at her. "Willa, what is it?"

She released a long, heavy sigh. It made the sheet ruffle a little at the movement.

"A thought was bothering me and I couldn't figure out what it was but now I know. But saying it feels like a not-so-cool thing to do given where I am and the fact that I'm very naked." It was one long, hurried statement.

Kenneth went from his side to sitting upright. "Whatever it is, you can tell me."

Willa also straightened. She brought the sheet along with her and covered herself.

She was self-conscious now.

Did she regret what they'd done?

Because he definitely didn't.

"I was thinking about you being tickled that I say the 'long way 'round,'" she started, not exactly meeting his eye. "Then I thought about you and everything we've been through, and then I thought about Ally." She let out a sigh of frustration this time. Then she was staring at him full-on. "I know this isn't the right time but… I mean I suppose there really isn't a *right time* to talk about it, but you said the day she was killed that she went out to the park to break in her new shoes, right?"

The entire conversation had caught him off guard but Kenneth nodded. "Yeah. She liked going to the park downtown. Before it was sectioned off into a dog park."

"The one off Main that backs up to the woods," she offered.

He nodded again.

"And she was found almost near the town limits, no-where near the park, right? But that wasn't where you thought she was killed?"

That look passed over her again. The one she'd worn when she'd been staring at the ceiling.

Deep thought. Not all of it good.

And she sounded like she'd been working on the idea for a while. How long had she been awake?

"Yeah. We never found the second bullet that went through and there wasn't…a lot of blood where she was. We expanded the search to include the park, though, and found nothing. Why? What are you thinking, Willa?"

She chose her words carefully.

"I had this friend in school who got these new running shoes and needed to break them in ASAP for a 5k she was doing with her boyfriend the following weekend. She wore them everywhere and, even though they hurt her feet, she'd insist we walk back to the dorms through the wooded path because it was hard terrain. She thought it would make the process easier or faster or something."

Willa angled her body so there was no mistaking where her attention was. "Maybe Ally did something similar and instead of staying at the park—"

Kenneth tensed.

Adrenaline shot through him.

An idea.

A thought.

A potential lead.

"Maybe she went the long way 'round because it isn't always about distance, it's about the challenge," he finished.

Willa nodded. "And if I was going to take the more challenging path from that park, and I'm also a local who enjoys going the distance with running, then I'd leave downtown and follow the woods up to the creek before coming right on back."

Kenneth threw the covers off him. He was out of bed in a flash and at his dresser looking for a new pair of boxers.

"That, if you kept in a relatively straight line, would put you really close to someone else's idea of a long way 'round," he said, words clipped and quick to maintain his excitement at possibly finding an answer. "Josiah Linderman's."

Willa was out of bed, too. She took the blanket with

her. There was no denying she was feeling the same energy he was.

"Exactly," she said, picking up on his thoughts. "And that can't be a coincidence, can it?"

"I don't know but let's go find out."

KENNETH DROVE TO the park while Willa laced up her shoes. Delilah was with them and she was picking up on their excess energy. The moment they left the park's old running path and went into the trees, she was all tail-wagging and sniffing.

Kenneth would have normally been more playful but he couldn't be now. Not when he was trying his best to think like Ally. He took every bit of knowledge he'd ever known about his late wife in the years they'd dated and the years they'd been married and moved through the woods at a slow but thoughtful pace.

Willa trailed behind him, quiet.

She was giving him space and, one day, he was going to let her know just how much he appreciated her thoughtfulness. And her patience.

Kenneth had a feeling that not all women would be keen on sleeping with a man only to go out the next day to look for the place his late wife had been killed.

Then again, Willa wasn't at all like most women.

Sure, she was sunshine and moonlight, but she was also so much more.

Someone he wanted to know more about.

But someone whom he let stay behind him while he became lost in another woman he'd cared deeply for.

That's how they stayed for half an hour or so. Kenneth moving across parts of worn paths and parts of the woods that he imagined Ally would prefer. He started to doubt that their lead was anything more than wishful thinking and, even if it wasn't, it had been years since her death. If they did find the spot where she'd been killed, there was a good chance they'd never know it.

They made it to the creek soon after he started to lose faith.

"She wouldn't have gone across it," he disclosed. "This is when she would have turned back."

Willa nodded and said she agreed, but didn't follow him right away. Instead, she went to a nearby tree. It wasn't dead, but there was a hollowed-out space at the bottom of its trunk. It looked as though an animal had made it into a den. Dirt, leaves and other debris had collected inside.

He paid it no mind.

But Willa did what Willa did best.

She surprised him.

He paused, watching her bend down.

When she straightened again, she looked caught between excitement and disbelief. She pointed down.

"I don't know why this keeps happening to me, but I've found another box."

It wasn't actually a box but a cigarette case. One of the fancy, vintage ones. Metal, with an intricate design on its top, it was ultimately worn and covered in grime. It had seen much better days.

Willa took Delilah's leash as Kenneth donned a set of gloves he'd brought with him, as always.

He paused to take a breath before opening the case.

He didn't know what he'd expected to see but a folded piece of paper and a small, whittled-down pencil wasn't it. He shared a silent look with Willa before setting the case aside and unfolding the paper.

It was a list of names. Ten in total. All but two had a cross through them.

Kenneth wasn't sure if the cigarette case was a clue to what they were searching for or just something someone had misplaced. Still, he read the names out, as if hearing them could give him some clarity.

"Grant Milligan. Terry Page."

He sighed. He shouldn't have let his excitement get the better of him. What were the chances that they'd actually find something after all these years?

Kenneth looked back at Willa to voice his opinion.

He stopped the second he saw how wide her eyes were. She didn't wait for him to ask her what had changed.

"If you think me finding that was a coincidence, wait until I tell you where I've heard one of those names before."

Two DAYS LATER and Kenneth was wearing a suit, a skinny tie, some boots, his badge and gun, and something akin to excitement across his lips. Willa watched him from the window of his SUV. She would have joined him but her own best-dressed self was trying to keep her heels dirt-free. Plus, in some way, it felt like Kenneth walking along Lot 427 was an intimate thing.

He was seeing where it had all started.

Just like she had when she'd first found the box.

It was night, timed that way only because they'd lost track of the clocks on their phones while going over their plan again.

A plan Foster Lovett wasn't happy about.

"Getting a warrant to search his house and work-place would be safer," he'd told them both that morning.

Kenneth had already thought about that.

"There's no judge in the world who would okay it," he'd said. "No matter what any of us think, the truth is we have no hard evidence. It's all circumstantial."

That was the understatement of the century.

Not only did they have no evidence that said Joseph Page—the same Terry Page who had been part of se-curing and championing for Lot 427 to be built upon—was responsible for murder, they had no idea which murder that was.

He wasn't old enough to have killed Josiah Linder-man...but his son, Joshua? Maybe. Since Foster had done his digging into Joshua, he'd found the number of the woman he had been dating seven years ago. Her name was Lottie and she'd told Kenneth a troubling story when he'd called her.

A few days before Joshua had talked to his uncle at his mother's grave, Lottie had all but broken up with Joshua.

"He loved me but couldn't seem to love the idea of committing to me," she'd told him. "I wanted to get married and have kids and he, well, he told me he didn't know if he could do that. So I told him he needed to figure that out and, if his answer swung our way, that he knew where to find me. He agreed to that and took his things and left. I guess he made up his mind. I never heard from him again."

From there Kenneth had said he'd been delicate when presenting the possibility that Joshua hadn't come back because something had happened to him. Then, when he'd asked after Joshua's adoptive parents and any friends or coworkers and why no one had reported the man missing, she'd rounded out the story with a deep sense of pity.

"His adoptive parents died two years apart from one another. After that he became very closed off to people. As for where he was working, he was between jobs. He wanted to be a journalist but was having a hard time getting hired."

Kenneth didn't say so on the phone but Willa had summed up his feeling after he'd recounted the conversation.

"Joshua really did just fall through the cracks, didn't he?"

The fact that his father had done the same thing weighed heavy on both of them.

Two Lindermans who had disappeared into nothingness.

Lottie had emailed Foster a copy of an old letter Joshua had given her after that and, at the very least, they'd been able to match the handwriting to the note in the cigarette case.

Had Joshua been investigating his father's murder as an adult? And, more important, had he found a lead that had brought him to Terry Page?

If so, then how did Ally Gray fit into it all?

There were too many questions still, and hunches that they couldn't back up.

So it felt like the only reasonable play left was to be a bit unreasonable.

And that's why Willa was wearing a party dress, why Kenneth was in a suit, and why Martha was waiting for them to drop Delilah off at her house.

They had a party to crash.

A party that Terry Page would be attending.

"What will that accomplish?" Foster had asked when they'd told him of their plan. "Are you just going to ask him if he's been killing people over the years?"

Kenneth had tensed. Willa knew the anger coming from him hadn't been meant for Foster but it eked out of his words.

"When I look him in the eye, I'll know if he's guilty."

Willa had known he was amped up…and emotional. It wasn't just about Josiah and his son. Ally was involved.

The one case he'd been forced to give up on.

So she'd pulled Foster aside when there had been a break in the conversation.

"If Terry Page is behind even one of these disappearances or, what we believe are in fact murders, then that means he's either the man from the hospital or he knows him," she'd said. "You know me and you know Kenneth. I can get Terry talking and Kenneth can guide that talk to something we can use. We have to at least try. If we show our hand to him first and he is guilty and we don't have a way to prove it? What's to keep him from running, or worse?" Willa had lowered her voice then. She'd looked toward Kenneth. Her heart had constricted and fluttered all at once. "He deserves answers. Just like Ally and the Lindermans, and *this* is the only way we can think of to maybe get some."

Foster had sighed but had agreed to the plan after that.

Though he'd been sure to point out it wasn't much of a plan all the way up until they'd left Kenneth's house.

"I'll be close," he'd called after them. "You say the word and that party will have more guests than they ever bargained for."

Willa found that image wildly comforting.

Though now she was starting to get nervous as she watched Kenneth and Delilah walk around Lot 427 like a man paying his last respects to a place before leaving it forever wasn't helping. They'd stopped on their way to Martha's at Kenneth's request.

If Terry Page *was* guilty, what would happen next?

What would she do? What would Kenneth do?

She watched as the man and his dog started to walk back to the car. His blazer was unbuttoned. Willa saw the glint of his gun beneath it.

For just a moment, Willa wished she'd never found the box.

And hoped that its discovery wouldn't take any more lives than it already had.

Chapter Twenty

The associates of Red Tree Development were celebrating two things.

One reason to have a party was that they'd just completed a long-standing project in a nearby city. Something, according to Ronaldo—the man who hadn't held back when talking to Willa on the phone after very little maneuvering on her part—that was a long time coming. It was a strip mall and, apparently, had been a pain in the entire company's collective backside over the last year. Closing the book on the property had been reason enough for celebration, yet they'd decided to be less obvious with their disdain for their work to share the party with an employee's birthday.

Her name was Wendy and her husband had a good bit of money when they'd married.

"Ronaldo said that's why, when Red Tree does decide to party, they usually do it at Wendy's place," Willa explained. They'd parked her car in a line of vehicles along a long drive. It wasn't McHale money but it wasn't some house out in the middle of town, either. "Not only is this place big, it apparently has dock access to the creek at the back of the property and a gazebo somewhere else."

Kenneth had cut the car's engine and quirked his eyebrow at that.

Willa seemed to pick up on his thoughts.

"Ronaldo seemed to like Wendy, but he had a lot of thoughts on people who own gazebos, and not all of them good," she said with a shrug. "Then again, he said if he had gazebo money then maybe he wouldn't dislike them so much."

Kenneth took the keys out and tucked his badge into his pocket. He wanted it on him if he needed it, but he didn't want to spook anyone until then.

"It's amazing to me how powerful your small talk is," he'd noted, not for the first time. "You call Ronaldo back to thank him for helping you and scoring points with your boss, and somehow you manage to get your-self an invite to a company slash birthday party with no one you know. *And* with a plus one." He shook his head and laughed. "It's a Southern superpower."

Willa wiggled her eyebrows at him.

"A superpower I'll use for good but don't think for a second I won't also use for it evil if it suits me."

Kenneth put his hands up in mock surrender and laughed.

Then the reason why they were there was staring at them through the windshield.

The house was large and set within the woods for privacy. Kenneth had only been by the home once when he was a teen and that was to turn his car around when he'd missed the dirt road to another dock access a few minutes before. He suspected since then the house had been renovated and given an addition or two. He also understood why Red Tree asked to party there and not at the office or a bar. It looked like something out of a movie. The two-story was lit up like a Christmas tree. Outdoor lights hanging from rustic-looking wooden poles every few yards led the way before the house lights inside and out took over. Music could be heard thumping, even before they got out of the car.

Two more pulled up behind them.

"I can't tell if it's a good thing or a bad thing that so many people are here," Willa commented. She'd lost her earlier humor. "Surely if Terry Page is our bad guy, he won't try anything with a crowd like this around?"

Kenneth grit his teeth for a moment. "He better not."

A sigh escaped Willa's chest. "Then let's get this thing going."

Kenneth caught her hand before she could reach for her door handle. Willa searched his face, confused.

But he wasn't.

Not at all.

"Willa, you already know that I don't like you being here—and *yes* I know you don't care because you're a strong, independent woman and the perfect 'wing woman' for this adventure," he said, loosely quoting her from earlier when she'd said her not going with him wasn't a negotiation. "*But* I have to say, I am glad you're with me."

They'd already shared a lot in the last week or so, including many intimate conversations between his sheets, but Kenneth felt the need and acute desire to share more.

He just didn't know how to say it exactly. Not when they were on the trail of a murderer. Not when they were fighting to hopefully find justice for Ally.

Not when there were so many unknowns that could still spell disaster for them.

So the short statement would have to do.

Though Willa didn't seem to take it lightly.

She took his chin, gave him a quick kiss on the lips, and broke it with a smile.

"For luck."

Kenneth returned the smile.

"Better than a rabbit's foot for sure."

They left the car without any further comment and headed to the house.

Willa took his hand before they went inside.

THE RED TREE employees and their significant others were a nice enough bunch. Willa vaguely recognized a few of them. She and Kenneth, dressed to impress, blended nicely, drinks in their hands and good company at their ears.

Ronaldo was there, all smiles. He pulled Willa and Kenneth into a friendly conversation that lasted several minutes with him and his husband. For half of those minutes, it all felt so normal.

But Willa caught a look across Kenneth's face that she probably hadn't been meant to catch. He might have been smiling but his eyes were like daggers as they surveyed the people around them.

It was a reminder for the rest of the conversation that they weren't on some fun double date. They were looking for a man with a thin-but-there connection to a box containing items related to two disappearances and one murder. Not to mention a cigarette case that held his name.

Terry Page.

Since learning his name, the sheriff's department had undertaken an in-depth investigation for information on the man. Unfortunately, he hadn't been listed in any criminal database and his social media profile had been scarce if not practically inexistent. The company's web site bio page had one single picture of him, but it was old and somehow managed to be absolutely unmemorable. If Terry Page wasn't guilty of something nefarious, he was guilty of online evasion.

Ronaldo and his husband suddenly excused themselves to take a call from their babysitter. Willa eased into Kenneth's chest and stayed close as she spoke so only he could hear.

"Ronaldo said everyone from his office is here, and that includes Terry Page. We need to mingle faster."

Kenneth nodded and then they were off. Sipping drinks, utilizing small talk and polite hellos, and passing compliments when sucked into someone else's orbit. It happened more than once and Willa could tell the routine was starting to wear on her partner.

It made her want to do something drastic to help his heart, which had to be hurting right now. He could, after all, be in the same room with the man who'd shot the woman he'd vowed to spend the rest of his life with.

Willa couldn't help the pain in her own chest at that truth. If Ally had never died, she never would have come to know Kenneth the way she had. Never felt the warmth of him, the rumble of his laughter, or the delight of seeing him joyful. She wouldn't be wondering about their future or if it would exist beyond the hurdles they were currently being thrown. She wouldn't have an affinity for Delilah and how much he loved her. And she wouldn't be standing in a crowded room of people fervently wishing to hold only one person's hand.

Willa knew in her heart that she would give it all up in an instant if she could somehow turn back time to save Ally.

Because that's how much she cared about Kenneth.

She wanted any and all of his pain to be replaced by unending happiness.

Willa sighed. She knew that was a pipe dream for every soul who walked the earth. That there would always be hard times. That happiness wasn't every second of forever. Still, she scanned the new room they entered with hope that they would at least find some helpful answers.

But there was no Terry Page.

There was, however, a familiar face that bobbed into view just ahead.

"Missy!"

Missy Frye and her husband were also dressed in their Sunday best and holding obligatory cocktails.

As they approached, Willa couldn't help but note that Missy's mass of curls put her own big hair to shame while Dave looked like he wished he was any-

Surviving the Truth

where else than in stiff clothes at some fancy-schmancy house party.

Missy dived in, bypassing any type of hello. "What are you doing here, Willa?"

Outside of Missy's calling the office to hunt down her husband, Willa only saw and socialized with her by bumping into her at places like the grocery store, hair salon, or any Clanton Construction functions. Missy was younger and had been more of Martha's crowd growing up.

Dave, though, wasn't a true local. A nice guy who had been down on his luck, he'd been passing through Kelby Creek when he'd taken a job as part of a construction crew. Instead of leaving, he'd married Missy quick and, as Martha had not-so-politely said, been her prisoner ever since.

To be fair, at the moment, he really did look the part of husband there against his own will.

"We were invited by a friend from Red Tree." Willa sidestepped a direct answer. She'd say Rolando if she had to, but wasn't sure why Missy and Dave were there at all. Missy worked in the county over at a nail salon and spa. So, Willa just asked, "What are y'all doing here?"

Missy was beaming. She'd been a social creature since she was in diapers, according to Martha.

"The same! And we just couldn't pass up the invite. Look at how stunning this place is!" She seemed to realize that Willa had someone with her and waited, pointedly, for an introduction.

"Missy, this is my friend Kenneth Gray. Kenneth, this is Missy and Dave Frye. I work with Dave at Clanton."

Kenneth was poised and professionally polite. He shook their hands, smiled like he was supposed to, and jumped right into a conversation about the almost-gaudy house around them.

Missy wondered aloud why the woman of the house would still be working if they clearly had money and Dave said that sometimes people did things that didn't make sense because outsiders didn't know the whole story.

They all agreed with him and Missy looked like she was ready to go another round of pure chatter when Kenneth pulled his phone from his pocket. Someone was calling him but Willa couldn't see the Caller ID.

Whoever it was, he gave her an apologetic look. "I need to take this."

Willa nodded and motioned to the next room. She hadn't seen anyone go in or out of it in a minute or so.

"Go ahead. It's fine," she assured him.

He excused himself from the group, saying it was work, with a quick squeeze to Willa's hand as he went. She watched him transform into downright focused as he hurried out of the room, answering.

Willa hoped it was good news.

She wasn't sure if they could take any more of the bad.

"Speaking of work, I guess this is as good time as any since your date isn't here, but do you think I could talk to you about one of our current jobs?" Dave looked downtrodden just bringing it up. "I was going to talk to you about it last week but you were out."

"For good reason," Missy added.

He nodded, immediately apologetic.

"Oh yeah, I'm not blaming you," he interjected. "I just mean that's why I didn't see you there."

Bless his heart, Dave had always been a somewhat simple man. He talked straight, was respectful, and became flustered fast.

Willa was more than happy to help ease his embarrassment, even if that meant talking about work at a party.

Being polite was in her DNA, after all.

"Don't worry about it. What do you want to talk about?"

A new song from the DJ in the main room kicked up. It wasn't as loud here as on the rest of the first floor, but it was annoying. Dave glanced at the door along the wall she presumed led out to the back.

"We can go outside, if that'll be easier for you?"

Dave nodded.

Missy huffed.

"I'm off the clock, so I'm staying inside," she announced. "Y'all just come back in when you're done. I'll tell Kenneth where you are if he comes back before you."

Willa thanked her and followed Dave outside into the night air. The lights hung out around the front of the house were sparse in the back. Though a path that led down a ways to what must have been the dock was faintly visible with lights in the distance.

If Ebony had been there she would have said, "You can't hide money."

But her friend wasn't there.

No one was really outside where she and Dave were.

It was good and private.

"So, what's up, Dave?" she asked, readying to try to help with whatever might be bothering him.

Dave set his drink down on the ground and looked back at the closed door. When his gaze went to hers, it had doubled down on apologetic.

So much so, she started forward, hand out as if she could help him with whatever it was that was weighing him down.

But then he spoke and Willa stayed right where she was.

"Missy shouldn't have called you that night. You shouldn't have gone out to the lot to look for me." He took a step forward. Willa had never noticed how big of a man he was until then. "And you should've never taken the box."

Before she could utter a word, move an inch or even scream, something hit her hard from behind.

Just as the world around her went dark, Willa had one last thought.

One day I've got to learn how to be a bitch.

Chapter Twenty-One

"One of our witnesses called in and said they lied about the man they saw at the hospital." Detective Lovett's voice was clipped and undoubtedly angry.

Kenneth made sure no one was in the room with him. It looked like a small office but without all the trappings of work. Just a desk, some nice chairs and a few wayward books. When he was certain no one would overhear him, he spoke.

"They *what*?"

Lovett talked fast. He was clearly on the move.

"The witness was one of the two people attacked on the second floor of the hospital to, as we assume, draw you and security away from Leonard Bartow's room. But before anyone could help, the attacker was able to say enough to scare both of them into giving a false description. Since they were the only people who got the best look at the guy, it was enough to tank our entire image of him."

"Did the witness decide to help us with a more accurate one?"

They'd been looking for the wrong man for days.

Kenneth swore beneath his breath in the space between his question and Lovett's answer.

"I did us one better. I sent him a photo lineup of sorts using several different people. He picked one picture out immediately as the man who was at the hospital. I just met with the second witness. I did some fast talking, and he agreed to cooperate. It was instant recognition with him, too. They both went for one man."

"Terry Page?" Kenneth felt like he was vibrating out of his skin in anticipation.

Lovett didn't make him wait a second longer.

"Terry Page," he confirmed. "That means we have enough to get him now and we're on the way. I'm ten minutes out. Deputy Park should be there before me. Play it safe and smart until we arrive."

Kenneth snorted. "Safe and smart can kiss my ass. I'm going to go find Terry Page and arrest him."

He ended the call, whirled around on his heel with all of the righteous vengeance in his chest, but came up short.

He hadn't heard the man enter the office, but he couldn't ignore the timing.

Or the strappy shoe that was in his hand.

It belonged to Willa.

Dave Frye looked sincerely regretful to be exactly where he was, but that didn't stop him from using a voice that was nothing but commanding.

"Throw your phone on the desk—and your gun, too," he said. He shook the shoe. "Or else this will be all that's left of Willa."

Kenneth's blood was boiling. "If you've hurt her—"

"Just put the gun and phone down, and we can talk."

Kenneth weighed his options. It was smart to keep his gun when Dave didn't appear to have any weapons on him. Yet, Willa's shoe brought him up short. He should have never left her. Even when he'd thought she was with friends.

He put the phone on the desk but hesitated with his gun in his hand. Instead of dropping it, too, he took the clip out and slid it into his jacket pocket. Dave watched with a raised eyebrow.

"So neither one of us can use it," Kenneth said.

It surprisingly didn't offend the bigger man.

Instead, his brow scrunched. When he started to speak again, it sounded like he was saying something he'd been forced to rehearse.

And Kenneth imagined he had been.

"You have two choices now. You can either die here alone or you can die outside with Willa."

Kenneth couldn't describe the anger that rushed through him. But he decided to bury it to keep the situation calm.

"Why are you doing this?" he asked, genuinely curious. If Terry had been the man who'd killed LeAnne and Billings, and Leonard had been the man who he'd fought at Willa's apartment, then how did Dave fit into any of this? "I thought Willa was your friend?"

The big man nodded.

"She is but friendship doesn't get you out of gambling debt."

"But murder does?"

Dave didn't seem to like that question. He made a disgusted face.

"I don't murder anyone. I only find things and then return them."

Kenneth wanted to point out that he'd just given one hell of an ultimatum for someone who didn't plan on killing anyone but realized then just how Dave fit into everything.

"You're the one who stole the piece of fabric from her apartment."

Dave didn't deny the accusation.

"It wasn't Willa's. It didn't belong to her."

It didn't make sense why Dave hadn't grabbed the box when he'd taken the bloody fabric yet, his ultimatum was still ringing clearly in Kenneth's head.

There wasn't time for any more questions.

The feeling must have been mutual. Dave's face hardened.

Apparently, Kenneth had been too swift to discount Dave. The bigger man reached into the back of his slacks and pulled a gun from its waistband.

"You die either alone or together," he reiterated. "Those are your only options."

WILLA WAS SICK right into the water. It was a miracle she'd even made it to the side in the first place—or maybe just instinct. Once she'd become conscious again, she'd heard the water, blinked against the dim lights strewed along wooden pillars, and had known if she got sick right where she was then her night would only head that much more downhill.

When she was done, the pounding pain in her head had only lessened slightly.

And the man who had dealt the blow seemed more annoyed than he would have been otherwise by the act.

"I didn't hit you that hard," he sneered. "You don't have to be that dramatic about it."

Willa wiped her mouth with the back of her hand. There was blood on it but she realized she must have grabbed at the spot on top of her head before passing out.

"You hit me hard enough to lose consciousness," she said with some added spice she hadn't realized would be there. "I'd say that counts as just painful enough."

Willa stood slowly and took a few steps back, trying to orient herself. She saw the path that led to the dock from the house again but, this time, from the other side. Somehow the house seemed farther than the dock had. She could hear the faint thump of music. She could also feel the wooden planks beneath her bare feet.

Her shoes were gone.

She took a shaky breath and finally met the eye of the man who had done this to her.

Terry Page looked as average as his name sounded. Apparently, his Red Tree bio picture had in fact done him justice. Short brown hair, brown eyes, clean-shaved. A man who looked as though he said things like "accounts receivable" and "return on investment" several times during his workweek.

Not a man who had become the center of a web of death and loss.

"We don't have much time," he said, smiling like it was a business transaction.

"Before what?"

He shook his head. "I'm not going to tell you that. Though, if you scream, I will kill you, hand to God." He moved his blazer and pulled out a gun, true to his word.

Willa wondered where Kenneth was and then hoped to high heaven that Dave, nowhere to be seen, wasn't with him. She didn't want to ask about the former in case there was any chance that Terry didn't know Kenneth was there with her. Instead, she did what they'd come here to do in the first place, even if it was under much different circumstances.

"What do you want with me?"

Terry sighed. Again, so average-looking of him.

"Well, to be honest, I really want to say I'm impressed with how you handled my initial mistake. When I first buried that damn box, I knew it was a bad idea. But I was in a hurry and Lot 427 wasn't even for sale, so I let that decision ride for too long. Then, when it finally went up, and I decided to try to retrieve the box, I realized I'd forgotten where I'd buried it." He snorted. "To be fair, it was a while ago and things were a bit hectic."

"So you convinced Red Tree to buy the lot for development. Why?"

He rolled his eyes. "It seemed like a good idea at the time. I'd rather keep my eye on the place than have someone else find it and take it."

Willa shook her head. It hurt.

She thought of Dave. Her heart squeezed a little. He'd

always been so nice to her. Yet, he'd taken her outside so Terry could attack her.

So Terry could kill her.

The only connection that she could come up with through her pounding head and fear was Clanton Construction.

"Is that why Dave is here?" she asked. "He was trying to find the box for you?"

Terry's nostrils flared. She could see it clear as day from the distance between them.

"Trying is the operative word," he growled out. "I had him looking for weeks and then you just stumble across it because his wife has control issues and needed to know where he was every second of every day. Ridiculous. Then again, I'm betting the rain helped you with that. There's just something about this town and flooding that uncovers things it shouldn't."

He took the smallest of steps forward. Willa wanted him to keep talking.

She also wanted answers.

"Is that why you sent Leonard to my apartment instead? Because Dave failed to find the box the first time?"

A look she couldn't gauge crossed over his face.

"Dave failed his first job, not his most important one." That confused Willa but he kept on before she could ask anything else. "But I did have the hope that hiring Leonard to get the box would work out but I guess strike two and three for outsourcing. I hired him to find the box, which he didn't, and then he went and got caught. So, I decided it was time to do things myself. Though, I admit things got a little sloppy."

He smiled like the cat who ate the canary.

"Like you killing LeAnne? Leonard and Billings too?"

Willa knew that Terry had been the one to kill them. Still, she needed to hear it.

He actually shrugged again.

"Like I said, things got a little sloppy."

Willa hated him. Right then and there she hated everything about him and everything he'd done. From the top of her hair to the tips of her toes.

"But why?" she asked, voice pitching higher. "Why go through any of the trouble? You didn't have a target on your back until you created all of this madness trying to get the box. You made yourself all the more suspicious. Nothing *in* the box even linked to you. If you hadn't tried to find it at all, we might not even have—"

All at once, Average Terry became enraged. He took two giant strides forward, which only made Willa shrink back that same distance until she was closer to the edge of the dock.

"Because I earned everything in that box. It's mine, no one else's."

Willa's heartbeat was all-out racing.

She hadn't expected that.

But she decided to use it.

She kept her voice as low and nonthreatening as possible.

There was something else that she knew in her heart

but, again, she wanted him to say it. First, though, she made sure her words were clear to lead him there.

"Because you killed Joshua Linderman and Ally Gray."

Terry's nostrils flared. When he laughed, Willa knew that she was beyond "in trouble." The man in front of her wasn't stable.

And had no intention of letting her go.

"I didn't kill them. I fixed his problems," he said. "Even after he died."

Willa didn't want to look toward the house but, at the same time, she was hoping to see Kenneth. Coming for her. Though she also didn't want him here. Not with the man who clearly had no problem killing.

"He?" she asked, hoping to keep him talking. The longer he did that, the longer she had hope of getting out of this.

Terry snarled, leaving any trace of his laughter behind.

"My father made a mistake over thirty years ago and here I am still correcting it," he snarled. "That's why the box isn't for anyone but me. *I* deserve it."

Willa took the smallest of steps back. A splinter bit into her foot. She didn't care.

"Josiah Linderman," she whispered.

That seemed to trigger the man more.

"My father thought he was untouchable. Getting drunk at home wasn't enough for him. He had to take it on the road. But then, there was Josiah, out walking." He clapped his hands together, the gun between them briefly pointed at her. Willa held in a flinch. "My father couldn't even handle burying the body. So, there I was at fourteen burying my first. I barely could lift him."

So, Josiah Linderman hadn't abandoned his family. He'd been killed by a drunk driver and then buried to hide the evidence.

"Joshua didn't believe his dad had left town," she guessed.

Terry snorted.

"I thought he did until he showed up at my house, asking questions about a piece of a car he'd found. Because, of course, my father couldn't be bothered to clean up his own mess."

"So you did."

He nodded.

"All I had to do was wait for him to go walking and follow."

Willa didn't say it but she believed Joshua had suspected the attack from Terry was coming. He must have thrown his theory, the cigarette case and the list, in the only place he'd time to—the tree in the small clearing in the woods next to the creek and not too far away from the back road his father had been walking.

Terry made another snarling sound.

"I shot him, but wanted to talk. So I made sure the shot wouldn't kill him fast, but we were interrupted."

Ally Gray.

"Stupid runner. Shot her after she hit me good. It's the only reason they got away."

That was news to Willa. Ally's body had been found, Joshua's hadn't. Had Joshua gotten away?

Her hope didn't last long.

And that had everything to do with Terry sensing he needed to crush it.

"Don't worry. They didn't make it far. Though Joshua sure was a pain to track. I'll give it to him, he made it a lot farther than I thought he would, but he made it easier, too. Buried him in the exact spot he asked me for mercy."

"But you didn't get to Ally in time?"

"No. She'd made it out to Becker's field and was spotted before I could deal with her."

He sighed, as if now bored.

"You shouldn't have taken the box, Miss Tate. It wasn't yours." His body language started to change. He was becoming angry again.

And it was all directed at her.

"The sheriff's department has it now and knows everything I do. Killing me, doesn't do anything."

He shook his head.

Willa's veins turned to ice. This was it.

Whatever he was planning to do, he was about to do it.

"Not true." His voice was like a knife dipped in venom. "It would make me feel better."

Everything happened in the space between heartbeats.

Willa turned around and dove into the water with enough force to go as deep as possible. Had it not been raining as much as it had, she would have gotten to the creek bed a lot sooner. Thankfully, it wasn't until she was completely submerged that a gunshot pierced the water behind her.

Willa kept her eyes shut tight and changed course as best she could. She was a good swimmer but when it came to holding her breath under water, she would never win any medals.

She struggled as another muffled shot sounded. She was going to have to surface soon.

Was she far enough away?

Had Terry been able to track her?

Would she be able to get back under to avoid being hit? Or could she escape through the other side of the creek?

Willa's chest started to burn. She started to swim up, terrified.

Even more so when something big splashed into the water somewhere behind her.

Willa kicked upward and broke the surface. She hoped the deep breath she'd taken in wouldn't be her last.

"Willa!"

She was seconds from submerging when she realized the man who yelled for her was Foster Lovett. He had his gun drawn down at a body on the dock. She could just make out the color of Terry's suit.

But who had jumped in after her?

"He's in the water, looking for you!"

Willa felt another flare of fear before the meaning sunk in.

"Kenneth!" she yelled, treading water.

It was like her voice was tied to the man.

One second it was just dark water. Then it was the face of the man she'd fallen in love with.

Kenneth was a few feet away but the moment he saw her, Willa could feel his relief.

"Willa," he breathed. "Are you hurt?"

She shook her head. In a fluid motion that didn't seem real, he swam to her and then pulled her with him to the other side of the creek. The minute his feet could touch the ground, his arms were around her.

"I thought he hit you before I got him," he said, still out of breath.

Willa noted his face had a few extra cuts and marks than when they'd arrived at the party, but she didn't focus on that.

Instead he needed to know that she was okay.

So she told him that she was.

Kenneth kissed her on the tail end of her words.

When he pulled back, he let out another sigh of relief.

"What's that one for?" she asked with a shaky laugh. Adrenaline was still surging through her.

"That kiss was for deciding to wear shoes that I could use as a weapon," he said, joining in with his own burst of tired laughter. "Dave never stood a chance."

Chapter Twenty-Two

Terry Page died on the docks. Kenneth had every reason to pull the trigger—to avenge his wife and to stop
a cold-blooded murderer once and for all—but the truth
was that he'd made the kill-shot for one reason and one
reason only in the moment.

To save Willa Tate.

Once he'd realized that she was okay, he'd taken a
minute to revel in that. Something made easier by the
fact that Deputy Park had found and detained the un-
conscious Dave in the house and that, true to Foster's
word, almost the entire department had shown up to
help.

Which worked out nicely considering everyone at
the party was confused and that confusion turned to
anger. Specifically, Missy Frye. After seeing her husband carted off in handcuffs, she'd attacked a deputy.

It would only be later that she admitted to him across
from an interrogation table that she'd had no idea about
her husband helping Terry do anything other than work
on his golf swing.

"They were friends," she'd tell Kenneth, still shell-shocked. "They're both good men."

Dave's own words echoed that sentiment when he was questioned later. Right before he told them everything he knew and had done.

"We met at the bar and, after some talking, Terry offered me a way out of debt. I couldn't say no to it. Plus, it wasn't much to ask. He wanted me to look for a box and then he wanted me to just focus on a piece of fabric."

When Dave had said that, Kenneth and Foster had shared a look. Foster had asked what Kenneth had been thinking.

"Why not take the entire box when you stole the piece of fabric from Willa's apartment? Why did he send Leonard in after you?"

"And why not tell Leonard exactly where the box was so he could find it when he did break in?" Kenneth had added.

Dave had seemed to think the answers were obvious and easy.

"When I went the box wasn't hidden. Well, I mean it was under her bed but easy to find. She must've hidden it later. And about the fabric, Terry said it was important to get it first so he might could have more time to deal with it before anyone realized it was missing. That wouldn't work if I took the whole box the first time."

"Why?" Kenneth had asked, genuinely confused.

Dave's answer had been simple.

Though wholly troubling.

"Because it wasn't his."

Kenneth and Foster had shared another look.

"Then whose was it?" Foster had asked.

Dave had shrugged.

"I don't know but he said he gave it back to the man it originally belonged to. I didn't ask past that and I don't think he would have told me had I done so. It's the only time I've seen him look nervous."

That was all Dave gave them but it was enough to send them back to the Page home to do another sweep, this time looking specifically for the piece of fabric.

They never found it.

"I think we just found our next possible new cold case to look into," Foster had said when they were done.

Kenneth didn't disagree but needed to put to rest everything—Terry Page first.

Natalie, Terry's wife, along with his coworkers had bucked and yelled about Terry being a good, decent man. No one had any idea that Terry was, in Kenneth's opinion, a sociopath. A killer. A man who was always one step away from deciding to end someone's life.

Those feelings, however, changed when Josiah Linderman's body was found in the backyard of the Page family home. He'd been wrapped in a tarp and buried deep. Terry's father, Kevin Page, had long since passed away but the medical examiner had found enough evidence to corroborate the story Terry had told Willa on the dock.

Josiah had been struck by a car and had most likely died instantly.

A week after his body was found, his son Joshua's was, too.

Though that had had nothing to do with what Willa

had learned out on the dock and everything to do with Lottie, Joshua's girlfriend at the time of his disappearance.

After Terry had confessed to killing Joshua, Kenneth had reached out to her because he felt that she deserved as much. They'd talked awhile about it all. At least, as much as he could, until Lottie told him a story about the first time Joshua had said that he loved her.

She wasn't from Kelby Creek and Joshua hadn't grown up in town, but he'd taken her out to his mother's grave a year before his death. He'd told her about how she'd liked this one spot where the honeysuckle grew so thick that it smelled like heaven on earth. Joshua had taken Lottie there and professed his love.

"He said he'd never been happier," Lottie had said, tears in her voice.

Kenneth had then asked where that spot was and, to his surprise, she'd remembered. Her directions from Mae Linderman's gravestone to her favorite spot in town had been spot-on.

Not far from where Ally had been found in the field.

Kenneth didn't take Willa with him when he went to check because he already knew that's where Joshua would be buried.

And that's where they found him, surrounded by honeysuckle waiting to bloom in spring.

The burial had been a hasty one, though, and among his things was a note that Terry had overlooked.

It was that note now that Kenneth held in one hand, the cigarette case that Willa had found near the creek in the other. Willa was at the window of his office, staring out at the parking lot. She was wearing church clothes and had even fixed her hair up into a complicated-looking bun. She wanted to look respectful but not too sad, she'd told him that morning standing in front of her closet wearing nothing but his T-shirt.

Kenneth didn't want to point out that once she read what was in the note, she wouldn't care what any of them was wearing, but he also realized Willa was trying to step away from her own emotions on the matter. There was no getting around that Joshua had left one hell of an impression with his last words.

She hadn't asked outright, but Kenneth knew that Willa had guessed his reaction at reading the note for the first time had been rough. In fact, he'd cried like a baby in Mae Linderman's favorite spot.

He'd tell her later but, right now, he wanted to be as professional as he could.

When Willa excitedly said Lottie had pulled up, he made quick work of seeing her into the meeting room. There, Willa gave Lottie a long hug before excusing herself.

She paused next to Kenneth in the doorway, surprising him.

"This is for you two," she said so only he could hear. "I'll come back when you're done."

And there she went, polite and true.

Then Kenneth began with the part of the story that Lottie didn't know and what the letter had helped fill them in on since the two of them had last talked.

"My wife, Ally, heard the shot and tried to help Joshua. From what we can guess, she hit Terry hard enough that it almost knocked him out. But not before he was able to shoot Ally twice."

Kenneth had a hard time with his words but managed to get through them. "After that, Joshua took them as far as he could before Ally couldn't go on. When he knew that he was getting close to dying himself, he left her body near a spot he thought would be found. He then went in the opposite direction, hoping that, if she wasn't found, he might be, so Terry wouldn't get away with it."

Kenneth slid the note over, along with the cigarette case.

Lottie laughed through tears in her eyes at the case.

"Joshua wanted to be an investigative journalist, you know? But instead of carrying around some kind of notepad, he put paper in that thing and golf pencils." She took the case and ran her finger over its top. "But this thing couldn't hold a lot, so the man was always stuffing paper and little pencils everywhere. It made doing the wash a nightmare. I can't count how many times we fought about it."

She laughed again then took a shaky, long breath.

At least now Kenneth knew how Joshua had gotten the paper and writing utensil.

"So this is the last thing he wrote?" she asked, looking at the note.

Kenneth nodded. "It's small, but he had enough time to say a lot. And it's addressed to you."

She touched it. Took another deep breath and shook her head.

"I thought he gave up on us. That he didn't want me anymore. I… I thought so many things about him since then. And now all of this? Can you— Can you read it to me? I… I can't."

Willa had warned him that, if she had been in Lottie's place, she might ask the same, so Kenneth was ready. As ready as he could be.

He straightened, smiled, and said sure.

Then he read aloud Joshua *and* Ally's last words.

"'Lottie,
'Terry Page shot me out by the creek. A lady named Ally, too. She tried to help me, but he was fast. We got away for a while, but Ally didn't make it long. I told her she shouldn't have tried to help, but she said she had no regrets in life and she refused to have any in death. Then she passed. I left her near the road. Hopefully someone will see her. But I'm worried he will, and will hide us all away, so I left. I decided that was a nice thought to die to…no regrets. But I have one—I should've proposed to you *already* but I was scared. I wish I hadn't been.'"

The handwriting had worsened as the note went on. Joshua had been dying and knew his killer might find him, so he'd finished the note with a simple thought.

"'I hope you live a long, good life, Lottie. Love,'"

Kenneth thought he probably meant to sign the note but had heard Terry coming and had hid it the best he could.

But not signing his name didn't take anything away from what he'd said.

"We also guess that this was on him when he passed. A jeweler in town sold it to him the day before. He said he was going home to propose to the love of his life."

He produced the engagement ring that had been in the box Willa had found. It had been Terry's trophy from Joshua just as Mae's picture had been from Josiah and the bullet casing had been from Ally.

Lottie took the ring. She started crying so hard that Willa appeared at her side with a tissue box and hand on her back.

Kenneth watched her try her best to soothe the stranger.

It would be a few weeks later that Kenneth would open up to Willa about the note and admit through tears that, without Willa, he would have never found out that Ally hadn't been alone when she'd died.

And that, to him, was the most peace he could ask for.

After Lottie left, Kenneth simply took Willa back to his house and put on a movie. He couldn't for the life of him remember what it was, but with Willa next to him and Delilah across his lap, he didn't much care.

She'd been staying at his place more and more and he was happy for it. Even though her apartment had been fully repaired and now sported a new security system, Kenneth felt a whole heap better with her at his side. Though, that had more to do with the woman herself than security concerns. Now Kenneth gave her a kiss on her cheek as she laughed at something that was said on the TV. She turned to him, cheeks rosy, and gave him a smile that put the rest of the world to shame.

"What was that kiss for?" she asked, hand absently stroking Delilah's fur.

Kenneth decided not to tell her that he'd just realized he wanted to spend the rest of his days like this, with her. So he told a little fib.

"For being warm," he said.

Willa laughed, caught his chin in her hand and pulled him in for another kiss.

Kenneth couldn't help the one word that came to mind at the touch.

Sunshine.

* * * * *

Look for more books in Tyler Anne Snell's Saving Kelby Creek series coming soon.

And if you missed the previous books in the miniseries, both Uncovering Small Town Secrets *and* Searching for Evidence *are available now, wherever Harlequin Intrigue books are sold!*

 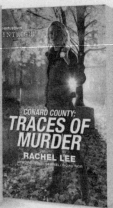

"What happens next?" Naomi had an awful, awful feeling that this was not going away anytime soon.

There were parts of no less than three people out there—of course it wasn't going away quickly.

"I've put in a call to the FBI office in Nashville. They're going to send a team to have a look around. Their crime scene investigators have far more experience and far more state-of-the-art equipment. If there's anything to be found, they'll find it."

The FBI.

The ability to breathe escaped her for a moment.

The sheriff held up a hand. "Don't get unnerved by the federal authority becoming involved. I know the agent they're sending, Casey Duncan. He's a good guy and he knows his stuff. The case will be in good hands with him."

"But why the FBI? Why not the Tennessee Bureau of Investigations?" Seemed far more logical to her, but then she knew little about police work beyond what she saw on television shows and in movies.

"Considering we have three victims," he explained, "there's a possibility we're looking at a repeat offender."

He didn't say the words, but she knew what he meant. Serial killer.

The queasiness returned with a second wind. "Serial killer?"

He gave a noncommittal nod. "Possibly. This is nothing we want going public, but we have to consider all possibilities. Whatever happened here, it happened more than once to more than one person."

She managed to swallow back the bile rising in her throat. "Should I be concerned for my safety?"

"I can't say for sure at this stage, but I'd feel better assigning a security detail. Just as a precaution."

She nodded, the movement so stiff she felt her neck would snap if she so much as tilted her head.

"We've focused our attention on the building where the remains were discovered and the immediate area surrounding it. The FBI will want to search your home. Your office. Basically, everything on the property. It would be best for all concerned if you agreed to all their requests. A warrant would be easy to obtain under the circumstances."

"Of course. Whatever they need to do." She had no reason not to cooperate. No reason at all.

"Good. I'll pass that along to Duncan."

Duncan. The name sounded familiar, but she couldn't place it. "He'll be here today?"

"He will. Might be three or four later this afternoon or early evening, but he will be here today."

"Thank you."

The sooner they figured out what in the world had happened, the sooner life could get back to normal.

She pushed away the idea that normal might just be wishful thinking.

How did a person move on from something like this?

They were talking about murder.

Don't miss
The Bone Room,
available October 2021 wherever
Harlequin Intrigue books and ebooks are sold.

Harlequin.com